THE SEANCE...

There was a sudden change in the medium's tone and attitude. No longer was she pleasantly conversational as she said:

"I have a strange feeling . . . ! With us tonight is someone alien to the peace of our circle . . ."

Timothy began moving along the row, careless of whether he was noticed or not. All eyes in the congregation were fixed on the medium. In a loud, almost harsh tone, she said:

"There is someone here who has no right to be here. I sense an evil influence. Someone among us is . . . *accursed!*"

The word hammered at Timothy's mind like accusations in a nightmare, transforming his mood . . .

THE HAND OF CAIN

Martin Thomas

PRESTIGE BOOKS • NEW YORK

THE HAND OF CAIN

First American Publication, 1967

Printed in the U.S.A.

PRESTIGE BOOKS INC. • 18 EAST 41ST STREET
NEW YORK, N.Y. 10017

1:
The Chiromancer

On the night of the first of the murders Matthew Lodway lurched out of the Nirvana Club into the summer dusk of that undistinguished university town, Stilford, and muttered a thick-tongued curse.

His mind was hazy from the succession of whiskies he had disposed of during the past hour. And among the alcoholic mental fumes simmered a bitter resentment of the way his plan for the night had been frustrated by a fellow club member. An opportunist who had neatly annexed his, Lodway's, feminine partner while he had been temporarily absent at the bar.

From the combined effects of alcohol and resentment Lodway was in no fit condition to drive. But, with his natural obstinacy, he turned left along the pavement towards the club car park where his Austin Healey was waiting, instead of to the right and the taxi rank which, in his present state, would have provided him with safer transportation.

After a few unsteady paces along the pavement he came to a sudden stop.

He stopped for one of the few reasons which, as long as he was actually conscious, could make an instant impression on him however drunk he might be.

The reason was a teenage girl, hurrying along the street in the direction opposite to his own. A girl whose elfin face he caught sight of in the yellow light of a street lamp, and whose youthfully feminine figure had first claimed his casual attention and then focused it into a deliberate inspection.

Now, turning to look after her when she passed by, he did move in the direction of the taxi rank. But it was the girl who was the magnet. The girl in skin-tight trousers and skinny sweater, with auburn hair reaching to her shoulders.

Those trousers emphasised her femininity as no skirt could have done. The tapering thighs they individually moulded impinged on his consciousness, proclaiming that the trousers had been specially made for a small-waisted, round-hipped, lissom female.

The sight, reinforcing the stimulating effect of the fresh air, began to dissipate some of his mental fumes. Temporarily banishing the thought of his car, he followed the girl. Past the taxi rank and along the extensive road of the town centre. To the fringe of the night-life area. The less exclusive fringe, catering for less expensive tastes than the club he had recently left.

Since beginning to follow the girl he had seen only four other people. Two young couples who had passed him without a glance, masculine arms round feminine waists, strollers immersed in their own interests.

Now Lodway had crossed an intersection into a street of coffee bars, a dance hall, a cinema and several amusement arcades. Here there were more people about. People of both sexes and of his quarry's immature age group. Shrill young females and uncouth young louts who made him suddenly conscious of his age. Even though he himself was only twenty-eight.

But age-consciousness alone caused his self-respect no twinges. His ego was not offended even by the decline from his usual social and intellectual environment involved in this brief hunt. Dukes saw no indignity in pitting their wits against those of a malodorous little fox classified by themselves as vermin. Lodway's own intended prey represented an objective that was classless—and any intellectual inferiority in that prey was as welcome to him as to a fox-hunting duke or a badger-digging rustic. Few hunters wanted a sport in which the odds were equal.

A couple of teenage rowdies now brushed by Lodway, staring at his face with challenging insolence. This was their territory. As much theirs as the din of a beat show or the long hair and wrinkled drain-pipe trousers which constituted their herd uniform.

His expensive orthodox suit, fashionable as it was by the standards of his class and age, set him apart as an unconforming intruder. Conspicuous among these young social "rebels" whose proudly proclaimed unorthodoxy consisted of a slavish, carbon-copy adherence to the crude and limited conventions of their dreary "pop"-culture.

Even Lodway's comparative erectness of carriage, despite his semi-sobriety, made him conspicuous among the surrounding examples of the round-shouldered, slack-kneed slouch that was another general characteristic of the males of the pop-nourished clan. As though they had been bred and born for the sole purpose of crouching over a guitar, that twanging emotional stimulant and mental bromide whose addicts outnumbered those of all other drugs combined.

Under that insolent inspection Lodway had to clench his hands with the effort to restrain his instantaneous impulse. An impulse to grab the two leering louts by their craning necks and crash their shaggy heads together.

But thought of the girl banished the impulse, and he

allowed the two young rowdies to continue on their slack-kneed way, unaware of his reactions.

The girl was now receding from him quickly, and he didn't intend her to get out of his sight. He didn't intend her to—but she did.

Fortunately he saw where she went. It was into the garish, neon-illuminated entrance of the "With-It Amusement Arcade." The title was slightly passé—as stressed by the more up-to-date "Switched-On Amusement Arcade" on the opposite side of the street.

But it was into the "With-It" that the girl had gone, so it was into the same arcade that Lodway went.

The walk in the fresh air had cooled his face and partly clarified his mental processes while leaving his zest for the chase at blood-heat.

The interior of the arcade made its name even more pathetic. In essentials the layout and equipment differed little from those of an old-fashioned pier funfair.

The customers were youngsters of both sexes, aged from about twelve to twenty. A juke box was blaring an aural assault which only a well-paid disc-jockey or the tone-deaf could find endurable. A rival amplifier was braying an invitation to the next Bingo session, with hooked optimists already seated at the counter on which the numbered cards were displayed, one card above each stool.

At one side air rifles were popping as equally optimistic marksmen tried to win packets of cigarettes which refused to be knocked over. Further along the large room a throng of noisy teenagers played the one-armed bandits. The only justification of the "With-It" title was an object securely bolted to the floor, for the use of children who frequented the place earlier in the day. This was a "space rocket" which offered a phenomenal journey into the stratosphere for the price of sixpence.

There was a foot-massage machine and, beside it,

another machine which would provide "beneficial" electric shocks. There was a machine equipped with a pivoting pistol by means of which cut-outs of cats could be shot off a painted wall.

There was a machine which supplied cigarettes and another which, although its peep-show pictures were colour photographs, was a direct descendant of that famous invention which had initiated the Edwardians into the secrets of What the Butler Saw.

At the far end there was a row of mechanical Chambers of Horrors, which were no modern descendants but genuine old originals hallowed with antiquity on many a seaside pier.

The crowd of teenage patrons was drifting in that direction, some to make a complete circuit of the offerings, others to make use of the rear exit into a parallel street. Many of them were sucking at straws dipped in Cola bottles, bought at a stall near the entrance.

Lodway was standing on tiptoe to look over the well-thatched heads for a sight of the girl he had marked down.

In this place her style of dress was the rule rather than an exception and he was afraid that unless he could get a direct glimpse of her memorable little face she would be unrecognisable.

Impatiently he thrust his way through the crowd, ignoring the scowls just as he ignored the general din. He passed the kiosk from which a gum-chewing young man was lethargically doling out small change for use in the slot machines.

Still no sight of the girl. Had she realised she was being followed and made a quick escape through the rear exit by means of a familiarity with the place? Lodway knew his own progress was certainly slower than the rate at which her slim and nimble body could have eeled its way through the throng.

But no. There she was! Same clothes and figure, same

auburn hair. Vigorously he forced his way on till he was alongside her and could see her face.

Despite the known popularity of that kind of sweater and trousers, he got a shock. The face he now saw was one he had never seen before. This wasn't the same girl.

Had the face been nearly as attractive as the one that had brought him here, he might have transferred his interest to this other girl. But her attractions were limited to her figure, and even the appeal of that was greatly reduced by the disappointing face above it. After the elfin little face which had arrested his attention, this other was deterrently plain. He was no believer in the adage that in the dark all cats looked grey.

He stopped where he stood. Till now he hadn't fully considered what he would do if he should catch up with the quarry he had followed. Offer her a Pepsi over at the refreshment stall? He winced at the thought. His tastes ran to something more sophisticated, mature, potent . . . private. A cosy setting in which he could overwhelm her with his adult charm. That well-tried charm which had made his experience in the Nirvana Club tonight a rare, and therefore keenly-felt, humiliation.

And suddenly that sense of humiliation returned in full flood. Tonight he'd been ditched by a woman of poise and discrimination. That had been bad enough. But it was even more humiliating to be standing here—futilely—among these gangling youths and scream-age girls en masse.

Success even with that little elfin-faced adolescent would have salved the evening's stings. But failure here too . . .

He felt that he was not only an outsider but an absurd interloper. Charming an impressed kid away from here for a ride in his Austin Healey would have been one thing. Standing here, conspicuous among the callow of both sexes, with nothing to show for his eager pursuit, was humiliatingly different.

And again he was being inspected. With one question obvious in the curious, amused young eyes around him. What was he doing here?

Flushing, he turned to avoid those subtly-mocking young eyes.

And then he found himself under the scrutiny of older eyes.

A pair of dark eyes peering at him from the curtained doorway of a wood-walled booth.

To provide himself with some recognisable object of interest under the teenage stares, he edged closer to the booth and looked at the advertising matter displayed on its front wall.

"*Madam Riva—Genuine Romany Palmiste.*"

Huh! So that was what the dark-eyed woman in the curtained doorway was. A fortune-teller. "Palmiste," hand-reader, chiromancer. . . .

Evidently business was slack and she had looked out in the hope of seeing some prospective customers. Probably she had instantly sized him up as a more likely potential client than the pop-obsessed adolescents comprising the bulk of the crowd.

Lodway gave a slanting smile. To give the curious kids time to lose interest in him, he casually studied a card displayed on the wall.

The card was obviously intended to impress the beholder with Madam Riva's professional expertise. It bore the traditional chiromantic diagrams of the left hand and the right hand, fingers and thumbs splayed.

Each hand was marked with the significant lines and zones, identified by the traditional labels of chiromancy.

The Lines of Heart, Head, Life, Fate and Sun. The Girdle of Venus, the Ring of Saturn. The Fingers of Jupiter, Saturn, Apollo and Mercury. The Via Lasciva and the Plain of Mars. The Mounts of Venus and Luna.

The diagrams ended just below the Three Bracelets of the wrist.

Looking at them, Lodway was suddenly deaf to the din about him. All his attention, almost his entire vital force, was suddenly concentrated in an eerie, frightening physical sensation.

The sensation that his own living wrists were encircled by burning bracelets of fire!

A wave of resentful disbelief brought a scowl to his face.

Mind over matter, he told himself. Real as the burning pain still felt, it was a ridiculous delusion resulting from his study of those diagrammatic hands.

Rubbing at his right wrist, he turned away from the booth, furious with himself for his mental suggestibility.

But still those kids were watching him curiously. Even more curiously than before, as if his face had betrayed his mental agitation.

Looking away from the young eyes, he again met the gaze of those older, gipsy eyes.

He braced his shoulders. All right. The exit of the arcade was still too far away to be reached quickly. Hemmed in here, he'd show these curious kids—and the watching fortune-teller—that he did have a normal purpose in coming to this place.

He'd let this idle "palmiste" have a bit of business—if only to get away from these adolescent stares. By the time he came out of the booth the gawping teenagers would probably have found something else to occupy their minds.

As he neared the curtained doorway the dark-eyed woman gave him a tentative half-smile of invitation and inquiry.

"Uh—yes!" he muttered, forcing an answering smile.

Nodding, she backed into the cubicle and he followed her inside.

Neither the palmist nor the interior of her booth had any resemblance to the stock gimmicks of the cartoon fortune-teller. There were no signs of the zodiac in the decoration of the room nor on the woman's dress. Madam Riva had the dark eyes, dark skin and black hair of a genuine gipsy, but she wore no gipsy ear-rings nor was there a kerchief over her head.

Her total professional equipment seemed to be a small table covered with a black velvet cloth.

She sat down at one side of the table and indicated the vacant chair at the opposite side. Lodway seated himself, conscious now of two things.

The burning sensation at his wrists had gone. And the din outside the booth was muffled. Possibly the walls were sound-proofed, the effect completed by the closing of the curtains. When the fortune-teller spoke, her words were perfectly distinct.

"One hand or both? One half a guinea, both a guinea. Both for the future. . . ."

"One will do," he said.

He gave her a ten-shilling note and sixpence. Then he extended his left hand on to the black velvet table-cloth.

The palmist was about to take his hand in her own two hands. But abruptly she hesitated, her dark eyes focused on his thumb. At the thick tip of the thumb.

Then her gaze flickered to his palm. The Head Line and the Heart Line. In his case, the Heart Line starting from the Mount of Saturn and with a series of minor lines running into it. Her fascinated gaze was held by a star just below the second finger, on the Mount of Saturn.

She shivered and drew away. Her gaze still lingered on his mind, as though against her own will, but she was leaning back from the table, her eyes and nostrils distended. As repelled as if his hand had exuded some noxious sweat or revolting odour.

Frowning, he stared at her face in angry wonder. She had become pale and her dark eyebrows were drawn together above her apprehensive eyes. She raised her glance to him with distaste. With positive repugnance.

"What's wrong?" he demanded.

She avoided his resentful stare.

"Nothing!" she said, in a flat voice. "I'll—I'll give you back your money. I—I don't feel well. . . ."

From her purse she brought out his ten-shilling note and a sixpence and edged the money across the table towards him.

"It's very sudden," he said, suspicious and with a deep anger beginning to smoulder. "But if you're as ill as all that . . . shall I ask someone to get you a doctor?"

"Doctor?" Her teeth showed in a startled, mirthless grin. "No. No . . . doctor. Just leave me. And don't come here again——"

"What?" He'd risen to his feet, scooping up his money. Her last words sparked his smouldering anger into a flame. "What the devil d'you mean by that? If you just feel ill——"

"That's all." She was evading his furious glare. "Go now, will you!"

As he turned to leave he saw her gaze following his hands in a kind of reluctant fascination. He felt his ears grow hot and a flare of anger surge up into his chest, almost choking him.

She wasn't ill. That was just an excuse. She'd taken a sudden dislike to him. A deep, intense dislike to him. Something she'd seen in his hands. The damned harpy! Who did she think she was? It was an intolerable insult. . . .

With anger almost stifling him, he kicked his chair away, turned and strode out between the curtains.

What a night! First ditched in the Nirvana Club. Then thrown off the track by that alluring little bird he'd had his eye on. Now a bare-faced insult by a fortune-telling fake in a cubicle!

A thought crossed his mind. Had she read in his palm the intention which had brought him to this amusement arcade?

No—that was nonsense. She was just a fake, able to bamboozle the credulous, and she'd simply realised that she wouldn't be able to fool him.

After all, for a fellow of his age, twenty-eight, any girl over sixteen was fair game. This amusement arcade was no Sunday School, anyway, and the fortune-teller's repugnance had been too deep to concern a bit of the girl-chasing that must be one of the favourite pastimes in this place.

True, when it came to the crucial point some females showed a strange lack of appreciation of their luck in having attracted his interest. It wasn't his fault that some of them had to be forcibly induced to see things his way—and afterwards bribed, blackmailed or terrified into silence. And even his methods of inducement and intimidation surely hadn't been so heinous as to justify the palmist cowering away from him as if in him she'd suddenly recognised some monster?

His evening was going from bad to worse. His score comprised two major disappointments and a couple of insults.

He was already feeling almost homicidal when, while making his scowling way towards the rear exit, he saw—the girl!

His sense of humiliation and anger instantly evaporated from the heated gust of another kind of feeling. This time there was no mistake! This time it was her face he saw and recognised.

With her back to the row of horror machines, she stood smiling among a group of girls and young fellows who had gathered in that corner near the exit.

What mattered now was to get close to her—and then make his presence known in a casual way as though he happened to be beside her quite by chance. Once the ice was broken, his looks, his smooth technique, his obvious mental and social superiority to her companions, would do the rest.

So that she should not see him making for her, he lowered his head and thrust forward through the crowd.

His hands tingled in anticipation of a satisfactory ending, after all, to this night of insults and frustration.

He had no inkling that, instead, the tick of the clock was marking his swift and inexorable approach to the first of the murders.

That he was hurrying to the fulfilment of the omens in those hands.

Omens of violent death!

2:
The First Killing

WHEN LODWAY looked up to check his progress, he had halved the distance to the group gathered round the horror machines.

But he had not halved the distance between himself and the elfin-faced girl. She was no longer among the group!

The bile of repetitive disappointment scalded hot in Lodway's throat. Tonight Fate was taunting him with the torture of Tantalus. Again and again, the wine cup at his lips—only to be snatched away at the last moment.

He peered above the crowd, questing to and fro for the girl like a hound that had lost the scent.

Then his eyes glittered! This time Fate was not taunting him after all. This time Fate was making it easier for him!

Because the girl had left the group in order to thread her way to the exit. And alone!

A pleased grin lived briefly on Lodway's face. She was leaving this arcade unaccompanied, and apparently without any idea that she was being followed.

Now he knew the way she was going he allowed her

to get to the exit before he moved again. Only when she had passed out of sight did he hurriedly force a way to overtake her.

He knew the street into which the exit opened. An alley in character, poorly lighted. In the shadowy recessed doorways of several buildings in the street, privately occupied couples were huddled, as indicated by urgent low masculine voices and occasional feminine squeals or giggles. The sounds did nothing to allay Lodway's sense of frustration and impatience.

The effects of the alcohol he'd imbibed were rapidly fading, but he was excited now by a different kind of intoxication.

Its personification was just visible, hurrying along the gloomy street. If she should continue in the same direction, it would eventually bring her to the river and its little-used towpath. A possibility which appealed to Lodway.

But she wasn't to continue to the river bank and its privacy. At least, not on foot.

As Lodway hurried to get within a reasonable distance of her, she paused at the intersection corner. And from the main road intersection stabbed a single bright beam of light. The light of a headlamp.

Lodway, too, paused to let it pass by. But it didn't pass. Instead, it swung across to the corner where the girl stood waiting, and into view came the solo motor-cycle which was its source.

Even as Lodway watched, the motor-cycle slowed then came to a stop at the kerb, beside the girl.

Lodway cursed. Then a lingering, persistent hope crossed his mind. Was this just some ton-up lout trying a casual pick-up? If so, it might be rebuffed.

But again—no. The rider looked like a ton-up kid, certainly, in his crash helmet, black leather jacket and tight jeans. But if this was a casual pick-up he was having undeserved luck.

The girl waved and ran to the bike. One of her tapering legs swung across the pillion seat. A pair of young arms went round the rider's waist.

Lodway's curses were soft, sibilant, corrosive. He sneered as the lucky rider took off his crash helmet, turned on his saddle and strapped the helmet on the girl's head.

"Gutter Sir Galahad!" Lodway mouthed with vicious envy.

The motor-cycle engine roared into renewed life. The bike moved away—carrying the girl who was never to know of a stranger's galled fury at the sight.

For long moments Lodway stood stockstill on the shadowed pavement, almost dizzy with the bitter frustration seething and scalding in him.

His hands were trembling and twitching as he turned to make his long way back to the Nirvana Club car park.

Where his Austin Healey awaited him—with no luscious young passenger to snuggle beside him.

When Lodway drove home, the mental rope holding his impulses in leash had frayed away to the last frail strand.

He was a very dangerous man.

Matthew Lodway was one of three brothers. The triplet sons of Virgil Lodway, Stilford's leading surgeon.

But though the brothers were identical triplets, with a strong physical resemblance to each other, there was no identity of personality, temperament and tastes.

Consequently only one of them had adopted the father's profession, and even he was so different from the old man temperamentally and intellectually that their careers had only the basic healing purpose in common.

Virgil Lodway, consultant surgeon at the Royal Hospital and lecturer in surgery at Stilford University, was a man of considerable professional prestige and financial standing. His researches and achievements in "spare parts" surgery were expected to win him a Nobel Prize.

Timothy Lodway's choice had been the medical profession, but in a much less ambitious way.

Timothy was a conscientious young general practitioner. Proficient and valuable in his routine career, but with none of his father's pioneer spirit and brilliance. Timothy was quite content as junior partner of old Dr. Dawson, with a prospect of some day succeeding Dawson as senior partner.

Alan Lodway was as conscientious and reliable as Timothy, and possessed some of his father's enterprise. But he had disappointed the surgeon by exercising his enterprise in his choice of career. Preferring music to medicine.

The father had derived some consolation, however, from Alan's evident musical talent and his dedicated zeal as first violinist in Stilford Philharmonic Orchestra. An orchestra with a reputation which was far from provincial.

Matthew was recognised by everybody, including himself, as the black sheep of the family.

He drew sardonic amusement from the knowledge that some people sympathised with him on that account. They were people who didn't know him very well and sentimentally thought of a black sheep as a misunderstood stray; a little wild, but only because of a warm heart.

They had such illusions because they hadn't seen him in one of his . . . outbreaks. Because they hadn't seen him with one of his victims. Female victims who—whether difficult or easy—inevitably aroused in him an eventual urge to maltreat and degrade.

He'd been very lucky to escape criminal prosecution over the varsity affair.

Stilford University had temporarily appealed to Matthew because it was co-educational. But that amenity had proved not only a persistent distraction from his studies. It had brought the end of them.

Only Virgil Lodway's influence—and the hard cash with which he had soothed the girl and her family—had saved Matthew from prosecution and an automatic gaol sentence. But not even Virgil Lodway's status at the university could have saved Matthew from being sent down, and the surgeon had had no wish to do so.

It was ironic that intellectually Matthew was the only one of the three sons who might have emulated their father's achievements as a research pioneer. The qualities lacking had been the necessary interest, industry—and what the old man referred to as "moral fibre."

It was a bitter pill for him when Matthew, having no degree, put his natural gifts to work in the field of car salesmanship. A pill made no more palatable when Matthew's commissions on sales soon brought him an income bigger than the combined incomes of his two brothers. Half an hour of slick sales talk on a demonstration run—spiced with masculine charm if the potential customer was female—could put more money in Matthew's pocket than Timothy earned in a week of day and night service to the sick. More than Alan earned in a fortnight after years of assiduous practice with the violin.

The odd thing was that, despite their temperamental differences and diversity of interests, the three sons continued to live with their father.

Timothy's profession made it understandable that he should do so. It enabled him to spend spare time talking medical shop and to call on his father's store of experience and more advanced knowledge.

Alan continued to live with them because he saw no point in taking a bachelor flat for the short time he intended to remain unmarried. If and when he moved it would be to set up a home with Alison Garfield, secretary of the Orchestra. There was an "if", because Matthew would not be surprised if even their matrimonial home should be a part of the old man's house. Alison already spent a lot of her time there, and the old man often hinted that she would be welcome as a permanent resident.

Matthew's own reasons for remaining there were mixed. One reason was the opportunities it gave him for exercising his sardonic humour on his brothers and to flaunt his bigger earnings under their eyes.

Another reason was that it also gave him a kick to keep the old man reminded of the black sheep of the family. A black sheep who had found himself some very nice grazing.

But the decisive reason, as he knew, was . . . Alison.

She was Alan's fiancée, and had several times reminded Matthew of the fact. But he hadn't abandoned hope of success in her direction—though he didn't intend that success to involve himself in a marriage ceremony.

He found it difficult to believe that any sane woman could really prefer Alan Lodway to Matthew Lodway. Alan might be quite a boy with a fiddle, but Matthew regarded himself as Alan's natural superior with that more subtle instrument, a woman. And he didn't need a printed score to tell him how to play.

The imminence of Alan's and Alison's wedding had no serious effect on Matthew's hopes. While he was waiting for Alison to grow tired of stodge and acquire better taste, there were other females to keep him amused; but he remained convinced that Alison would eventually find Alan tedious and welcome Matthew's interest in her. If only *after* the wedding!

At the worst, Matthew calculated, a few months of close domestic contact with Alan would be enough to give Alison a yearning for someone less dreary. Meanwhile there was always a hope that she would see sense even before getting tied to the worthy fiddler.

For her Matthew had an intense and abiding passion, in which even that elfin-faced little teenager would have been only a superficial, transient interlude. It was, in fact, because of a slight resemblance to Alison's piquant features that the teenager had appealed to him so much.

Matthew was still scowling when he drove home in the dim and diffuse light of a moon partly veiled by a thin layer of cloud.

He was scowling when he drove through the open gateway of the big Lodway house in the exclusive suburb of Crestleigh.

The tree-dotted grounds of the house were quite extensive. The long drive was a pale ribbon between the grass-grown areas shadowed by trees and shrubbery.

Driving round to the garage beside the house, he saw on the concrete wash-down the mini-car owned by Alison. So she was here again!

The only car in the garage was Alan's, so Timothy and their father were out. The cook, daily woman and gardener-handyman had gone home hours ago. Which meant that the engaged couple had the house to themselves.

Matthew gave a sardonic grin. It would be a pleasure to butt in on their cosy little twosome!

He went indoors. Alan and Alison were not be be seen. Surprised, he searched the house. With a suspicion he would not previously have associated with stodgy Alan and prim Alison, and with a consequent mounting jealousy, he even extended his search to the bedrooms.

Still no sign of them. Where the hell were they?

Strolling in the grounds, perhaps? Yes—that was more their mark. Dreamy musical types strolling hand-in-hand and murmuring drivelling abstractions under the ghostly moon.

He went downstairs, and outside. He walked round the house, peering and listening. He passed the handyman's work-shed and the greenhouses. Still no sign. . . .

Then his questing gaze caught sight of the tip of a

pointed wooden roof, just visible above some distant shrubbery.

Was that where they were? In the summer-house?

Of course! With the seclusion and the padded seats, where better to sit and dream and plan and primly canoodle on a warm summer night?

With the pleasing thought of shattering the idyll, he went along the tarmac path towards the summer-house. Creeping stealthily in the shadows cast by the surrounding bushes and trees.

Almost soundlessly he reached one of the unglazed windows of the circular wooden structure. He peered in. By now his eyes had adapted themselves to the dimness and enough moonlight filtered into the summer-house to tell him that his search was over.

To show him something that gave stinging revival to his sense of frustration and brought the bile of jealousy boiling up into his tight throat.

As far as his contemptuous anticipations were concerned, the joke was on him.

The slight sounds he himself had made when approaching would not have mattered. Not only would they have been inaudible to the two people in the summer-house because of their own hard breathing and rustling movements, but those two people were much too intimately engrossed with each other to have ears for anything as stealthy as his approach.

Alan's and Alison's occupation was neither abstract nor prim. Far from dreamily planning the future, they were actively enjoying the present.

To Matthew for a strange moment, because of the physical resemblance between the brothers, it was like watching himself in the rôle he had so often envisaged with Alison. Then came the bitterly mocking realisation that the rôle he was actually playing was the ignominious one of *voyeur.*

But he felt no sense of shame or compunction in playing it. It was a warped satisfaction to him that Alan and Alison did not have the privacy they imagined. With the further satisfaction in prospect of humiliating them with his eye-witness knowledge of the interlude. Or even using it to induce Alison to share the privilege with the eye-witness.

The spectacle concentrated on them his deep and vicious urge to vent the venom of his evening's experiences. For him an evening of insults and frustration, climaxed with the insufferable humiliation of being *voyeur* to Alan's . . .

And with Alison!

His recent contemptuous, patronising thoughts now mocked him with their maddening inappositeness.

And, to rub salt in the lacerating fact, it was the frustration of his own plans which had sent him home in time to witness this. Had he not been deprived of the girl at the Nirvana Club, had the elfin-faced teenager not eluded him . . . he would not have reached home till long after this summer-house interlude was over.

As it was, Alan evidently knew that his father and Timothy were out, and assumed that Matthew would not be coming home till his usual hour of one or two in the morning.

Abruptly, Matthew turned away from the window and stumbled back on to the tarmac path.

His face was livid, his mouth was twitching and the fingers of his two hands writhed together like intertwined snakes.

But when he got back to the house he was outwardly composed. In the lounge, without switching on the lights, he helped himself to a cigarette and dropped into an easy chair. With his elbows on his spread knees, he stared into the gloom, his mood brooding and black.

It was three-quarters of an hour later that the whirr

of a car starter brought him out of his sombre reverie. The sound was followed by the purr of a motor, which gradually faded away along the drive.

A couple of minutes afterwards Matthew was dazzled when the room lights came on. In the lounge doorway stood Alan, staring across at him in surprise.

"Hey—didn't know you were home!" he exclaimed.

Still seated, Matthew looked up balefully.

"Too true you didn't!" he said.

Alan frowned in puzzlement, then crossed to the cocktail cabinet and poured himself a drink.

Glancing at Matthew's bloated face, he said: "I won't ask if you want one. You look as if you've had enough already."

"Could say the same to you," Matthew leered. "And not about booze!"

"Eh? What the——"

"That was Alison driving home just now?" Matthew inquired. "Contented with her evening, I trust?"

Alan took a sip of his drink and then put the glass down on a table.

"What are you getting at?" he demanded. Still with that puzzled frown, but now sounding a little uneasy under his brother's taunting and suggestive grin. "Yes, she's just gone home."

Matthew's grin became nastier.

"Never mind. She'll be here again in a day or two, and there'll be plenty more where that came from."

Alan stared at him.

"You'd better go to bed," he suggested. "You're drunk."

"I've had a drink or two, but I'd have preferred the other. We haven't all been so lucky this evening——"

Alan's face flared red. His eyes glittered. He came closer to his seated brother.

Quietly he said: "You'd better explain what you mean!"

Matthew gave a scoffing laugh. "Oh—please! Be your

age. Music hath charms to . . . *fire* the maidenly breast . . . huh? Even prim little Alison's!"

"You swine . . . !" For a long moment Alan stared down at the mocker. "You damned peeper! You've been spying!"

Matthew's laugh was harsh. "There was no 'Keep Out' sign on the summer-house. So I just went to it without ceremony . . . like you and Alison!" Another laugh. "So you couldn't wait for the wedding ceremony, eh? Well, I'm the last bloke to blame you. But if I'd known little Alison was so forthcoming, I'd have tried my own luck with her!"

"You treacherous snake! I understand you already have!"

Matthew shook his head from side to side, leering.

"Only tentatively. But when I see Alison in a day or two she may be a little less frigid towards a man who's seen just how . . . torrid she can be!"

Alan exhaled a long breath.

"You'd try blackmail too, eh?" A slow smile creased his face. "Well—you're going to be out of luck. The Orchestra starts a three-month provincial tour in a fortnight's time, and tomorrow Alison goes on in advance to make the board and lodging arrangements. Then she'll be coming with us on the tour, so she said goodbye to Dad and Tim this evening. And when we come back from the tour we're getting married. So you're stymied, you lecherous——"

Matthew shrugged.

"You think a wedding ceremony will cramp my style?" he jeered. "You think you're the only man Alison will be easy for . . . now?"

Alan paled.

"I see . . ." he said softly. "Thanks for letting me see into your festering mind. Alison and I had intended to live here after getting married—but if you're going to be here we'll live somewhere else. Even if I have to join an orchestra in another town. I'll see you don't get your hands on her, you slimy ram!"

As the frustrating facts had hammered home, Matthew had flinched in his chair. But now that last frail strand of his civilised self-control snapped.

With his powerful hands groping, he came up out of the chair and made an animal-like leap at his brother.

The sheer savagery of the attack swept Alan off-balance. He crashed down on his back with those groping hands at his throat.

Matthew's face was now contorted into a devilish mask of homicidal hatred.

"You're not going to take her away!" he snarled. "You're not going to keep her to yourself. You're not going to have her again . . ."

With each threat he drove those club-tipped thumbs deeper into Alan's throat.

Alan was gasping, his arms and legs threshing. Already his oxygen-starved body was weakening under that terrible grip. His fingers were already too feeble to dislodge it.

His face was swollen, empurpled. His eyes were bulging horrifically from their sockets. All that came from his gaping mouth were those hoarse, choked gasps and a dribble of saliva.

"You're not . . . !" Matthew mouthed. "You're not . . . ! Die, damn you! Die . . . !"

His fair hair dishevelled, his distended nostrils working, he crouched astride his brother's writhing body, his teeth exposed in a ghastly grin of evil triumph.

Alan's struggles were rapidly growing feebler, feebler. His floundering had almost stopped. His bloodshot eyes were staring in blind agony.

For several more age-long moments Matthew maintained his murderous grip. Suddenly Alan's body went slack, inert. His tormented chest no longer heaved. His breathing had ended.

Even now Matthew continued the strangling grip . . . till quite sure that the body under him was lifeless.

Then he straightened up from the hips, his face dripping sweat, his hands shaking.

He was about to climb to his feet when sounds impinged on his rioting consciousness. Footsteps.

Slowly his head turned. His glowering eyes were wary. The door opened. In the aperture stood Virgil Lodway, father of the two men in the room.

The surgeon remained at the doorway as if paralysed. His incredulous, horrified eyes were taking in the macabre tableau.

Then he came a slow step forward into the room. And his accusing voice came in a harsh, remote whisper.

"Cain!" he said, in that terrible voice. "Cain! You've killed your own brother!"

Sullen-eyed, breathing jerkily, Matthew Lodway looked down at his guilty hands.

The first of their murders had been committed.

3:
A Butcher Calls

VIRGIL LODWAY finished his examination of his dead son and got to his feet. His pale features as impassive as some stone carving, he faced the other son.

Matthew stood watching sullenly, warily. His killer hands hung at his sides, but even now their fingers were hooked as if ready to fasten again on human flesh. Virgil Lodway did not miss the fact.

Glacially he said: "You deserve to hang. If you weren't related to me and Timothy, I'd hand you over to the Law!"

Matthew's hands moved very slightly forward.

The surgeon gave a bleak, unintimidated smile. "If you kill me too, you'll make certain that the Law gets you——"

Tense, waiting, Matthew retorted sullenly: "Why should I harm you?"

"Why should you have harmed your brother?"

"We—we quarrelled, and I lost my temper. He provoked me——"

"You've often provoked your brothers—but they didn't murder you!"

Only a man familiar with death in its ugliest forms could have remained as self-controlled as the surgeon. Only a man remembering his third son, now absent, could have remained so logically dispassionate. Could have kept in mind the possible repercussions of this tragedy upon the innocent.

"You don't understand——"

"I understand that one of my sons has died at the hands of a brother. That the son lying dead had a promising career—and his wedding day only a few months ahead."

"I'm—I'm sorry——"

"That would be an appropriate remark if you'd knocked over someone's glass of beer. It's a life you've destroyed. And only one fact is going to save you from the Law. The fact that the work being done by Timothy and myself is more important than legal punishment for you. Alan is dead. Nothing can alter that. What matters now is that Timothy's work and mine shan't be ruined by the scandal of a fratricide in the family."

Virgil Lodway moved quickly across the room and drew the curtains. Turning to face Matthew again, he said:

"If the truth about Alan's death became known, I would have to leave Stilford and so would Timothy. How many patients do you think he would keep if it was known that one of his brothers was a murderer?"

"You're going to tell him?"

"No. I can't be sure how he'd react. Anyway, it wouldn't be fair to burden him with such knowledge."

"You're going to let it be thought that . . . Alan was attacked by some intruder?"

"Certainly not. There must be no suspicion of foul play. No inquest, no investigation—no murder hunt. And there's only one way to avoid those things. Alan's death must be certified as due to natural causes."

Matthew's rigid attitude relaxed a little. His expression became less sullen.

"By you—or Tim!" he muttered.

His father's mouth twisted.

"I doubt whether Timothy would perjure himself on your account—when the victim is his brother!"

Matthew said rapidly: "It was an accident. I didn't really mean to harm Alan—not seriously." He kept his gaze averted from the inanimate thing that had been his brother. "I just didn't realise . . . he didn't resist as much as I expected——"

"A fact of which you took full advantage! But leave the talk. Help me carry your brother up to his bed before Timothy gets home."

Even for the surgeon it was a gruesome procession out of the room and up the stairs, with the murdered body carried between father and son—and that son its killer. But Virgil Lodway said nothing as they laid the body on the bed. When they left the bedroom he locked the door and dropped the key into his pocket.

Down in the lounge again, he said: "You should be glad your father didn't waste his opportunities and become a car salesman. Alan died of a cerebral haemorrhage. Fatal apoplexy. That's what's going to be certified."

Matthew stared at him. "By you?"

"No. The Law has reason to look askance at certificates of sudden death signed by the next of kin of the deceased. Timothy's partner, old Dawson, is a friend of the family and virtually the family doctor. I'll phone him my diagnosis and ask him to sign a certificate to that effect."

"Won't he ask to see the . . . to see Alan?"

From Virgil Lodway another bleak smile. "An insignificant G.P. risk offending one of the country's leading surgeons by asking to verify his diagnosis? You know how proud he is of having a son of mine as his partner!"

Matthew shrugged. "That'll really be the same as signing it yourself, won't it!"

"In effect, yes. But not in appearance, which is what matters. Alison will have to be informed of Alan's death, of course, and she'll hurry back. To her, apoplexy will be a plausible explanation of his facial appearance, if she insists on seeing him. But Timothy must be prevented from making a close examination——"

The surgeon stopped. There was the sound of a car approaching along the drive. He moved to the door.

"I'll make sure if it's Timothy," he said.

He went out. Matthew heard the car engine cut, then he heard the low murmur of voices. This continued for a couple of minutes.

When the surgeon came back into the house he was accompanied by Timothy. Timothy white-faced and shaken.

"One knows such things happen . . ." Timothy muttered, looking from his father to his only living brother. "But Alan—without warning! Who was here at the time?"

His father answered. "No one but Alan himself. I found him—lying dead there on the carpet. Matthew came home soon afterwards. When I went out this evening Alison was here with Alan. Obviously he must have had the seizure after she'd gone home—or she'd have done something about it."

Timothy brushed a hand across his forehead.

"Where is he?" he asked dully. "Can I see him?"

"We took him up to his room," the surgeon said. "I'll come with you."

Anxious not to miss Timothy's reactions, Matthew followed the two medical men up the stairs.

After unlocking the bedroom door, the father led the way to the bedside and stood between it and Timothy.

From a couple of yards' range Timothy stared down at the distorted face. The throat was concealed by the sheet drawn up to the chin.

"Poor Alan!" he whispered. "And just about to be married. . . ." He made to edge past his father. "Can I examine him?"

Virgil Lodway said harshly: "Why? I've already told you the cause of death. Are you questioning that? Please remember he's your brother. I won't have you treating him as a post-mortem specimen!"

Timothy stepped back quickly, scarlet-faced.

He stammered: "I—I didn't mean——"

"Then please leave things to me. All you need do is to bring the certificate from Dr. Dawson after I've phoned him the cause of death. I'll see to all other arrangements. I can afford to miss a few lectures, but there's no need for you to neglect your patients."

The surgeon turned to regard both his surviving sons. "You two go downstairs," he said sombrely.

Timothy, making allowances for the old man's grief, followed Matthew down to the lounge.

As dawn approached, Matthew sat alone in his room, thinking.

He knew now that he could depend on his father to do everything possible to conceal his crime. Even if it necessitated hiding any throat bruises from the eyes of the undertaker's men. Since the surgeon had decided on his course of action, Matthew had faith in his ability to deceive or over-awe lesser experts. He had already given ample evidence of his willingness to do so.

But Matthew's satisfaction in that regard was shadowed by a very uneasy thought.

That gipsy fortune-teller!

Had she foreseen, in his hand, the likelihood that he would be involved in murder? And would she remember his face?

Because when the evening paper came out with the report of Alan's death, it was fairly certain to accompany it with a photograph of Alan. And Alan had had a strong facial resemblance to Timothy—and to the brother who had consulted Madam Riva!

Would she remember that client's appearance well enough to notice a resemblance to a newspaper photograph of a man who had suddenly died? And would what she had seen in the client's hand make her suspicious of his double's death?

Or—would she think it was he, the client, who had died?

No. The paper would mention that Alan Lodway had been one of triplet brothers. So if the fortune-teller should remember her client's appearance she would allow for the possibility that he was a brother of the man reported dead.

And even if she wasn't suspicious about the death, the news item would provide her with the surname of the client who had been so repugnant to her. If she noticed his resemblance to Alan Lodway's photograph, she would have an indication of the repugnant client's surname—and address.

She had paid much more attention to Matthew's hand than to his face. But what details of his facial appearance that she *had* noticed would probably have been fixed in her mind by the strong feelings his hand had aroused in her. So there was a distinct possibility that if she should see Alan's photo in the evening paper she would be reminded of the client she had sent away with a repugnance amounting to horror.

And Matthew didn't relish the idea of the gipsy palmist knowing the name and address of that client—and perhaps henceforth looking out for further news connected with him, in case it should fulfil whatever she had seen in his hand. Even if she didn't regard the report of Alan's sudden death as a fulfilment of what she had been expecting . . . !

A press photograph of Alan wasn't the only possible source of danger.

On his professional rounds, Timothy necessarily met a lot of people. It was always possible for him to come under the palmist's eye—and for his resemblance to her distasteful client to acquaint her with that client's identity and the sudden death in his family.

It was equally possible for her to meet Matthew himself again while he was moving about the town on his work. With murder on his conscience, that was another possibility which did not appeal to him.

There were altogether too many dangerous possibilities inherent in the gipsy palmist's continued existence!

Matthew felt his hands tingling again with a strange excitement. He knew now precisely what he had to do. It would be pointless for his father to go to such lengths to save him from exposure if a nasty-minded fortune-teller were left alive and able to stir up dangerous suspicions. He, Matthew, really owed it to the old man and the family good name to prevent such a possibility.

It was his obvious duty to find Madam Riva—and ensure that she should not take an interest in one of the surviving Lodway brothers.

If he could catch her at home before she left for her stint in the amusement arcade. . . .

He was not afraid that she would be expecting him. A clairvoyant might have done. But he knew enough about the various methods of fortune-telling to realise that no psychic faculty was necessary for the practice of palmistry. Like astrology, it was claimed by its practitioners to be a science, which could be taught and learned.

Madam Riva might have seen murder indicated in his hand. But she would not have had any clairvoyant visions of the victim or victims, nor any detailed precognition of his thoughts and plans.

Without bothering about breakfast, he drove into Stilford a couple of hours later, to trace Madam Riva's home address.

To do so was absurdly easy. A small poster beside the entrance of the amusement arcade notified the hours at which she could be consulted. Evenings in the arcade—and mornings at her home address. The latter being a caravan on the outskirts of Stilford.

It was a luxurious modern caravan. Unfortunately for Madam Riva, it had the surrounding field to itself. It was also unfortunate for Madam Riva that when Matthew arrived her window curtains were still drawn. Because she did not see who her visitor was till she had opened the door in response to his knock.

Obviously she had been roused from her bed, because she had dragged on a housecoat over her nightdress.

Her reaction when she saw him at the door made Matthew glad that he had not banked on her having a poor memory for faces. The dark eyes which scanned his face widened with recognition and the same strong revulsion she had exhibited before.

Matthew's quick jump into the caravan rushed her back against the bunk from which she had just risen. As though of their own volition his now-practised hands found her throat and closed in a deadly constriction.

Unlike Alan, she had no illusions about the attacker's capabilities. But, being a woman, she was able to offer little more resistance than Alan had done.

When the gasping and the writhing had stopped and her body slumped slackly in his grip, Matthew laid her out at full-length on the bunk. He confirmed that the heart-action had ceased.

After pulling on a pair of thin gloves he searched the caravan for money or other valuables. Best to provide an obvious motive for what was obviously a murder.

A small cashbox contained a wad of pound and ten-shilling notes. He unlocked the box by means of the key suspended from her neck on a thin gold chain.

The notes, obviously her professional earnings, were not numbered in sequence and would therefore be safe to use. But Matthew decided that he would dispose of them by means of a little fire in the grate of his room. He wasn't hard-up for money. He would be content with having taken the fortune-teller's life.

When he drove back to his father's house his hands were no longer tingling. Steady on the steering-wheel, they were temporarily appeased.

They had efficiently and ruthlessly committed their second murder.

As efficiently as if specially designed for the job.

Alison arrived hurriedly at the Lodway house in late afternoon.

"It's—it's unbelievable!" she burst out, facing Matthew and his father in the lounge. "Alan was perfectly all right when I left him last night——"

The surgeon shook his head.

"Outwardly, my dear," he said gently. "But how could you foresee the rupture and haemorrhage of a cerebral blood vessel? That can strike as suddenly as lightning."

"But—what brought it on?" Alison asked, in bewilderment.

Virgil Lodway said: "Obviously the blood vessel concerned must have become weakened. But the precipitating cause——"

Watching Alison closely, Matthew put in: "As I understand it, apoplexy is brought on by violent emotion or exertion—or both. Could that explain it?"

With his gaze on her, Alison paled—then flushed vividly. Matthew's eyes glimmered with satisfaction. Had he made her feel that she had been a contributory factor in Alan's sudden death?

In a subdued voice she asked: "Can I see him?"

Gently Virgil Lodway answered: "If you insist, my dear. But I wouldn't recommend it. Apoplexy can cause severe facial contortion, and I think it would be better for you to remember Alan as you last saw him."

Matthew said: "Yes—just as he was when you were with him last night!"

The surgeon frowned, sensing some undercurrent of innuendo which he did not comprehend.

Alison's shoulders sagged. Dispiritedly she said: "All right. You know best. But I'll be coming to the funeral, of course."

"Can I drive you home?" Matthew offered.

"Yes—you do that!" his father agreed. "You shouldn't drive in that nervy state, Alison. Go home, take a sedative and go to bed. You've had a terrible shock."

On the way out to her little car Alison's control broke. As Matthew helped her get in she was sobbing.

But while he was driving her to her home near the centre of Stilford his own mood was one of considerable satisfaction.

Here Alison was, close beside him. Alison now unattached and with a vacancy in her life to fill. How long before she would welcome consolation from another man? And who better than one of her late fianceé's brothers?

If it was true that one was predisposed to fall for a certain physical type, whom was Alison more likely to fall for now than someone with a strong physical resemblance to the man she had lost?

Matthew deposited her on her doorstep, garaged the mini-car for her and left without seeking to prolong his time in her company. To have made himself a nuisance now would have been fatal to his long-term plans.

Before getting a taxi to run him back to the Lodway house, he bought an early edition of the evening paper.

As he had anticipated, the news report of Alan's sudden death was accompanied with a photograph. Quite a good portrait of Alan.

But it wasn't going to trigger off any dangerous thoughts in the mind of the palmist who had found his brother so repugnant. Instead of seeing that photograph, the palmist had her own death announced in the same edition.

Only a brief paragraph in the Stop Press.

PALMIST TRAGEDY

Stilford palmist Jane Smith, professionally known as Madam Riva, was found dead in her caravan at mid-day today by her butcher, when he called to make a delivery. Foul play is suspected and the motive is thought to have been robbery.

Matthew Lodway read it with a sardonic grin.

Appropriate that it was her butcher who had found her dead body. Because it was "her butcher" who had preceded him at the caravan.

A butcher of two human beings!

The hands responsible for the butchery crumpled the newspaper and tossed it into a litter bin.

On the way home in the taxi, satisfied that he was now safe, Matthew allowed his thoughts to revert, with pleasurable anticipation, to the girl in need of consolation.

When he replaced Alan in her life, there would a piquant additional satisfaction in the knowledge that it was he himself who had created the vacancy!

"With these hands . . ." he hummed gloatingly, suffused with an intoxicating, sadistic joy as he visualised Alison's fair, yielding flesh at last in their irresistible grasp. . . .

4:
Grim Atonement

On the day after Alan's funeral Timothy, concerned about his father's state of mind as a result of the bereavement, called at the University to give him a lift home in his car instead of the usual taxi.

Matthew had resumed his sales job and was still living with his father and surviving brother. Unknown to Timothy, this was because the surgeon considered it wise to keep Matthew under his eye as much as possible.

As Timothy's car threaded its way through the traffic of late afternoon the two medical men carried on a desultory conversation.

After getting free of a long traffic jam Timothy drove along a fairly clear road in a district of terrace houses and small factories.

"Just one call to make here," Timothy said, stopping the car beside a row of houses adjacent to a timber merchant's yard. "Won't be long!"

"No hurry," Virgil Lodway said abstractedly. Most of his leisure thoughts now concerned Alan.

Timothy kept his promise. After being inside one of

the houses less than ten minutes, he reappeared on the doorstep, came down the path and began to walk back to the parked car, his professional bag at his side.

He was diagonally crossing the pavement when his glance passed casually into the open gateway of the nearby timber yard. Next second he dropped his bag, turned and ran into the yard.

Greatly surprised, his father climbed out of the car, picked up the dropped bag and put it on the backseat of the car. Frowning, he turned towards the timber yard gateway, wondering whatever had made Timothy dash inside so precipitately. With the steadier pace appropriate to his age, he himself approached the gateway.

What had sent Timothy into rapid action had been the sight of a young boy's dangerous antics.

None of the timber yard workmen was in view. But in front of a big storage shed stacked high with planks of wood was a bench equipped with a circular saw. Timothy had both seen and heard that the saw was in motion. He could hear the whine of the blade as well as the sound of the motor driving it.

But even the sight of a circular saw left in operation and unattended would not have fired the young doctor with such urgent anxiety. What had done so had been the sight of a boy, aged about ten, who was leaning over the saw bench and tossing blocks of wood at the spinning blade.

The way the wood blocks bounced off the blade was the lesser of the dangers—though the boy might easily be blinded by some of the flying splinters.

On the sawdust-covered ground there were scattered piles of such blocks of wood of various shapes and sizes—ends sawn off battens and planks. The boy was perched insecurely on a few of these blocks, having a private and highly dangerous game in the absence of the workmen.

If the boy should lose his precarious balance on those blocks he was likely to be flung face-forward on to the bench—right into the spinning teeth of the mechanical saw!

To save him from this danger, Timothy ran across to the boy and grabbed at his jacket to yank him away.

He got a grip on the jacket, but to do so he himself had to tread on the scattered wood blocks.

Steadying himself momentarily, he exerted his strength to throw the boy aside, away from the saw bench.

Yelping, the boy staggered away from the danger zone, to land on hands and knees.

But immediately Timothy released his grip, the force he had exerted was no longer counter-balanced by the resistance of the boy's weight. Inevitably, relieved of that weight, Timothy reeled forward off-balance.

Even then, had he been standing on firm ground he might have recovered his balance. But his feet tried in vain to maintain a balance on the irregular layer of discarded blocks.

He sprawled forward head-first towards the saw bench. In an automatic reflex his hands shot out to break his fall and obtain a grip on something secure.

But between them and the bench top was the spinning steel saw, its teeth a blur of vicious speed.

Timothy's scrabbling hands met the serrated edge of the whining saw. His scream tore through the dusty air.

His hands were not even cleanly severed. They were mashed.

While his shoes floundered helplessly for a foothold, his frantically waving hands swept back and forth across the saw blade to a shower of blood, flesh and bone.

The terrible damage was done in seconds.

Timothy's wild, agonised shrieks brought Virgil Lodway running through the gateway and three timber-yard men racing from sheds and woodpiles.

The boy Timothy had saved from danger was crouching on his knees, gibbering in terror at the bloody horror on the saw bench.

Before anyone could reach him, Timothy flopped clear of the saw. He sprawled limply to the ground with his hands dragging a crimson trail across the bench from their gory tatters. From the wrists gouts of bright-red arterial blood spurted in twin fountains to the rhythm of his heart-beats.

He was unconscious from shock when Virgil Lodway joined the workmen gathering in helpless stupefaction around him.

From his pocket the surgeon quickly dragged a large white handkerchief and twisted it into a rope. Swiftly he bent to tie it around one of Tomothy's forearms, inserting a ball-pen to twist it tight.

"Any of you have another?" he jerked out. "For a tourniquet? Any first-aid man here——?"

"Here he is!" one of the workmen said, hoarse with agitation.

Two of the men were averting their eyes from the spurting globs of flesh and bone that had been hands. Their faces were slightly green.

A new arrival joined the group.

"I'm the first-aid man——" he announced quickly.

Virgil Lodway said crisply: "Help me fix tourniquets, then get gauze dressings for the hands——"

As the first-aid man improvised a second tourniquet and another man switched off the saw's driving motor, someone else said loudly: "I'll phone for an ambulance——"

With the tourniquets now fixed and the arterial blood no longer spurting, Virgil Lodway paused for a badly needed breath.

Accustomed to thinking rapidly and decisively in the midst of surgical crises, he now frowned in brief thought.

Then he called: "No! No ambulance. I'm a surgeon and this is my son." He turned to the first-aid man. "If you'll help me get him home, I can give him the necessary attention."

The first-aid man looked dubious.

"Seems irregular, sir——"

Impatiently the surgeon produced one of his professional cards and thrust it under the man's nose. The qualification "F.R.C.S." made an instant impression.

While the gauze dressings were being applied the yard foreman belatedly appeared. His questions were quickly answered by his men.

"If one of you can drive——" the surgeon suggested.

"Me, sir!" the foreman offered. "You just tell me where!"

"Excellent!"

Six minutes later the foreman was driving Timothy Lodway's car to Crestleigh, with Timothy in the back, lying across the knees of his father and the first-aid man.

He was unconscious, in shock, his face as white as paper.

On the journey, Virgil Lodway mentally consolidated the outrageous idea that had come to him while he'd been kneeling above the mutilated body of his son.

The foreman took the car up the drive and brought it to a stop in front of the house.

To the first-aid man the surgeon said: "I've a private operating theatre and laboratory here. If you'll help me carry him there——?"

"Of course, sir!"

With the foreman going ahead to open the necessary doors, Timothy was carried to the laboratory-cum-theatre in which his father had originated and performed many of his advanced surgical experiments.

Timothy was laid on a surgical table. Straightening up, the surgeon took two five-pound notes from his wallet and handed one of them to each of the two men.

The foreman flushed. "No need of that, sir!"

"No," the first-aid man agreed. "Helpin' the injured is what I'm for."

"Take them," the surgeon insisted. "And phone for a taxi to fetch you back to your work."

"All right, sir," the foreman said. "Seems this son of yours saved that young boy, but it's cost him——"

The first-aid man broke in: "Before I phone for a taxi sir, I'd better phone for an ambulance too, hadn't I? Or another doctor? After all, you being his father an' on your own here——"

Over Virgil Lodway's face flickered a very strange expression. Then he said something which would have amazed Timothy, had he been conscious to hear it.

Something which would even have frightened Matthew, had he been present to hear it.

The surgeon said: "This injured son of mine is a car salesman. But I've another son who's a doctor. He lives here and will be home soon. I'll get him to give me a hand!"

And as he spoke, in his anguished eyes showed a subtle glimmer of implacable determination and macabre mirth.

When Matthew Lodway arrived home an hour and a half later, his father came out of the house to meet him.

Even before getting out of his Austin Healey, Matthew could tell from his father's expression that something was seriously wrong.

Virgil Lodway broke the news with matter-of-fact simplicity.

"Timothy has had an accident," he said, walking beside Matthew into the house. "You'd better come and see him."

"Accident? Where? How?" The questions came in staccato bursts.

The surgeon didn't answer them.

"He's in my operating theatre," he said, leading the way to it. "I've been giving him some emergency attention."

They went through the research laboratory and Virgil

Lodway opened the door of the operating theatre. The room was brightly lit, strictly functional in design and equipment, with enamelled walls and rubber floor. Matthew's questing glance immediately fixed on the wheeled table on which was lying a motionless human figure.

A shape covered up to the chin with a blanket. From one arm a rubber tube rose to an inverted drip bottle suspended on a high stand.

The surgeon did not go across to the unconscious man. Instead he led Matthew to a trolley on which was a stainless steel tray. He pointed to two things lying in the bloodstained tray.

They were two little heaps of mashed flesh and splintered bone, partly blackened with congealed blood.

Suddenly pale, Matthew stared down at them.

Virgil Lodway said starkly: "Those were Timothy's hands. I had to amputate them."

Matthew put a hand over his mouth and quickly turned away.

His father said: "You need a drink."

Matthew hurriedly followed him out and down to the lounge.

There his father said: "Sit down. I'll get you one."

With his back to Matthew, he stood at the cocktail cabinet, pouring the drink. Turning, he came back with a half-full glass, which he gave to Matthew.

Matthew took a greedy gulp at the diluted brandy, then asked: "How did it happen?"

"It happened because Timothy saw a young boy in danger and saved him from it. The . . . accident was Timothy's reward. An unjust world."

From under hooded eyelids the surgeon watched till Matthew had emptied his glass. Then he took it from him and returned it to the cabinet. Again he came back and stood looking down at his seated son.

"A bad job," Matthew said perfunctorily. "But there are pretty good artificial hands nowadays, aren't there?"

"There are," his father confirmed. "I'm glad that fact consoles you."

Something in his tone made Matthew stare up at him in puzzlement. But even as he stared, Matthew's eyes became glazed and fixed, as though out of focus. He spoke, but his voice sounded thick and weary.

"Funny . . ." he said, brushing a hand across his eyes. "I'm feeling . . . tired . . . sleepy . . ."

"Then sleep!" his father said sardonically.

For a fleeting instant a spasm of suspicion glinted into the glazed eyes. Then the eyelids closed and Matthew's chin dropped on to his chest. He slumped in the chair, breathing stertorously.

When he awoke, his brain could not at first interpret the visual sense his opening eyes registered. Then he realised that he was lying flat on his back, gazing up at a ceiling. At something circular set in it, immediately overhead.

A large lighting unit, its perimeter a series of mirrors to eliminate shadow.

He tried to sit up—and found that he couldn't move. His head twisted. His eyes widened with fear.

He was wearing pyjama trousers and was bare from the waist up. He was lying on an operating table—and was strapped down on it.

His mouth opened, but all that emerged was a croak.

Again his gaze went down the length of his body, to his strapped ankles. The hair at the nape of his neck stirred to a spinal chill. He was wearing long, thick, woollen operation socks!

Wildly he looked to and fro, searching for an explanation—but dreading it.

There was another table a yard away from his own, bearing the unconscious figure of his brother Timothy. The blanket had been removed and Timothy too was bare above the waist. His bare arms ended in thick pads of surgical gauze.

Matthew's glance continued to dart in all directions. To the steriliser, now steaming for use. To the distant pedal-bin, placed ready for swabs. To the instrument table, with its rows of frightening stainless steel instruments. Scalpels, saws, forceps, clips. Needles and sutures. . . .

Then his field of view was filled with the sight of a standing figure, looming over him. A tall figure clad in a green surgical smock. From under a green surgical cap a stern face looked down at him.

A face as stern as that of some ancient patriarch about to exact a blood sacrifice.

"W-what——" Matthew babbled. "What's this——? Why am I——"

Coldly, Virgil Lodway said: "I mentioned that it's an unjust world. But sometimes its injustices can be rectified!"

"What d'you mean? What's that got to do with——"

Implacably the surgeon said: "Only one of my sons now has hands. You—who least deserve them. You, who put them to the most evil use—the murder of your brother!"

"Father! I—I——"

"You owe a debt to society, and that debt you are now going to repay in some measure. Through Timothy. You are about to make partial atonement for the murder of one of your brothers—by sacrificing part of your physical faculties to your other brother!"

Matthew glared up in incredulous horror.

"You're mad!" he said huskily. "You can't mean——"

"I mean that you are now about to receive condign punishment, for the benefit of your surviving brother—who lost his hands because he cared about other people."

The surgeon glanced down at Matthew's strapped arms.

"Those hands of yours have been misused to destroy life. Timothy used his to save life. It would be an ironic injustice for a wastrel such as you to have hands while Timothy's services to humanity are hampered or ended for lack of them!"

Matthew's mouth was dry. His body cringed.

He said hoarsely: "I know you've done wonders in spare-part surgery. But even if you can do it, it will be a crime. And why pick on me?"

Inexorably the surgeon said: "Picking on you is a matter of necessity as well as poetic justice. Even you know that the body will not accept a graft from an unrelated person. It will accept a graft only from an identical twin or triplet. People have been known to make voluntary sacrifice of a bodily organ to restore the health of a twin brother or sister. Such a voluntary sacrifice is not to be expected of you. So I am imposing it on you!"

Almost hysterically, Matthew cried: "It's an abominable crime! You'll go to gaol for it!"

A bitter smile. "If I do, so will you! Are you prepared to denounce me to the police—and then have to stand trial yourself for the murder of Alan! Believe me, if you ruin Timothy's career, I shall have no mercy on you. You should feel flattered to know that Timothy will be putting those hands of yours to better use than you have ever done. You'll have to take consolation from a fact you yourself mentioned. That very good artificial hands are now available——"

Matthew almost sobbed: "You know I meant for Timothy——"

"Yes. For him, artificial hands would be good enough, eh? They will have to be good enough for you. All you really need for your work is a glib tongue. You'll still have that. Now . . ."

The whites of Matthew's eyes showed all round the irises in a glare of horror. Into view his father had just brought a hypodermic syringe.

Softly he said: "It's going to be a difficult double operation for me—with no theatre staff to assist. No anaesthetist but myself. But I'm going to succeed. This is going to be the climax of my work. My finest feat of surgery. . . ."

The syringe came down to Matthew's bare left arm, its needle poised.

Through a haze of terror, his father's voice reached him. Pitiless, sardonic.

"Before you go under, take comfort from another injustice. You will get the credit for saving that young boy at such a cost. It's necessary for it to be thought that it was my car salesman son who suffered the accident—so that there will be no suspicion of how you actually lost your hands. Keep still. . . ."

Matthew had little choice about that. The straps prevented him from moving as the needle was pressed expertly into his arm and the piston was driven home. He croaked in frantic, futile rage. He was in the middle of an incoherent profanity—when unconsciousness swept down on his brain again like a black velvet curtain.

5:
The Little Swami

When the midget accosted him, Matthew Lodway was standing alone at the bar of the Nirvana Club, brooding.

Near his black-gloved artificial right hand was a glass he had nearly emptied of its scotch-and-water. His black-gloved artificial left hand awkwardly held a cigarette.

Awkwardly as the cigarette was held, the feat represented a good deal of ingenuity on the part of the makers of the hand and an achievement of hard practice by Matthew himself.

Nearly a year had passed since that night when he had been robbed of his natural hands. Only recently had he become accustomed to the artificial replacements with which he had been fitted as soon as possible after the double amputation. But even now, compared to hands of flesh and bone, these man-made substitutes were crude and limited.

His father's monstrous action had necessitated quick planning to cover up what had been done.

The day after the amputation of his hands, Matthew had been taken to Stilford's best nursing home for further treatment and the subsequent fitting of the artificial hands. His father "explaining" that he himself had naturally performed the essential emergency operation of amputating the hands "ruined beyond repair by the circular saw."

In the nursing home it had been very little consolation to Matthew to find himself the object of sympathy and admiration because of the way, it was accepted, that his crippling loss had been sustained.

The young boy he was believed to have dragged away from danger at such personal cost had been brought to see him, to express his regret at that result of a warm-hearted action.

As the boy had had only a glimpse of Timothy in the timber yard—lying injured and surrounded by men—he obviously did not suspect that the patient recuperating in the nursing home was not his rash rescuer. Matthew resembled Timothy in facial appearance far too closely for any such suspicion to arise. And the bandaged stumps where Matthew's hands had been were the stark identification labels of the victim of the unattended saw.

Timothy had to be taken away from Stilford for his grafted stolen hands to heal. To accompany him and supervise the union of the grafted tissue, his father had claimed the sabbatical year's leave from the University which was overdue to him. He had installed Timothy in a rented bungalow in Bournemouth.

He had not allowed Dr. Dawson to see Timothy before they left. By telephone he had told Dr. Dawson that Timothy had suffered a sudden nervous breakdown necessitating immediate sedation, rest and privacy.

Twins and triplets were known to be in close rapport with each other. Timothy's breakdown was evidently a delayed reaction to the sudden death of his brother Alan, reinforced and brought to a crisis by Matthew's terrible accident. Timothy would need a long rest from work and it would be advisable for Dr. Dawson to engage a temporary assistant pending his return.

Timothy's departure from Stilford was made necessary by the fact that "Matthew's" accident was common knowledge in the town. Obviously it could not be revealed that both the surviving Lodway brothers were simultaneously afflicted with wounds involving the hands.

Matthew had been quite pleased at his father's and brother's absence from Stilford. His hatred of them both was so virulent that he wanted no reminders of them. Neither did he wish to live with them again on their return. So he took a small flat not far from the town centre. And not far from where Alison Garfield lived.

He resumed work before Timothy was able to do so. The car firm transferred him to a desk job as assistant sales manager. Sympathy and admiration for Matthew brought many orders, with proportionate commission for the handicapped man with whom the sympathisers wished to deal.

Timothy's return to Stilford brought Matthew further financial profit. Timothy had felt shocked and guilty on discovering what had been done by his father. He had written from Bournemouth to tell Matthew so, enclosing a cheque for a substantial amount to help Matthew with his financial needs.

Timothy was evidently unaware of the threat by which his father had secured Matthew's submission to the situation. When he returned to Stilford and came to see Matthew, the man whose hands he now possessed did not enlighten him. To do so would have involved confessing to the murder of Alan.

Distressed as Timothy was about the situation, there was nothing he could do to improve it. He couldn't compel his father to regraft the hands back on their original owner. Nor, as Virgil Lodway had pointed out, could he denounce his father and so cause a sensational scandal which would inevitably wreck both their careers. All Timothy could do was to continue to help his handicapped brother financially.

The sight of Timothy using the hands stolen from him had at first caused Matthew a surge of palpitant hatred of such intensity that he had nearly blacked-out from vertigo. But he too could do nothing about the situation.

Murder his father or brother—or both?

Virgil Lodway had taken precautions against such a reaction from Matthew, killer of one relative.

Before driving Matthew to the nursing home his father had given him a double warning. That should Timothy die suddenly the police would be informed of the facts about Alan's death—with a suggestion that Timothy's death should be investigated as another probable fratricide.

Further, should Virgil Lodway himself die suddenly an envelope he'd deposited with a new solicitor would be handed to the police. The envelope contained the factual information about Alan's murder—and a suggestion of the probable cause of his father's sudden death.

Having made that icily clear, Virgil Lodway had intimated that he would not be ungenerous to Matthew financially as long as he "behaved himself."

So Matthew had had to content himself with cheques from the two people he now hated more than he had ever hated anyone, even Alan. He hated them more because there was no apparent way of venting that hatred.

And for hating Timothy he had more than one reason. The additional reason being—Alison Garfield!

Living fairly near her now had enabled him to meet her "accidentally" in town once or twice. Since the loss of his hands there had been a perceptible change in Alison's outward attitude to him. She was one of the many people who had expressed admiration of his impetuous concern for the young boy in danger, and regret for what it had cost him.

But he knew that those sentiments, though sincere, were strictly impersonal. That it was only because of his misfortune that Alison tolerated him on the rare occasions when they happened to meet.

These chance meetings were usually in the Lodway house at Crestleigh, when he had called to drop a hint that another cheque would be welcome. His physical presence with his artificial hands evoked a more generous response from Timothy than a phone call might have done.

Alison still made occasional visits to the house, ostensibly to see Virgil Lodway, who had so nearly become her father-in-law.

What gnawed at Matthew was the question: was that her real and only reason?

He had anticipated that, after losing Alan, she might eventually be ready to fill the gap in her life with one of the brothers who so resembled him. Was that the real motive of her visits to the Lodway house? A wish to keep in touch with the only one of Alan's brothers still living there?

Timothy!

When he thought of it—and thought too of Tim's present physical advantage over him—Matthew cursed and sweated in jealous, impotent hatred.

He was in such a mood when the midget accosted him in the Nirvana Club.

The voice came to Matthew from such a low altitude that it startled him. From below the level of the bar; below the level of his own waist.

The voice was soft, smooth and sibilantly accented. It said:

"Do not be so sad!"

Startled out of his morose introspection, Matthew looked down towards the floor—expecting to see some half-sloshed joker crouched on hands and knees.

Being in no mood for such juvenile frivolity, he was about to utter a blistering notification of the fact—when he saw the source of the softly-spoken words.

His peering glance met the steady gaze of a pair of eyes at about the level of his hips. But the owner of those eyes was standing. Standing upright.

He was a midget. A midget of less than three feet in height!

That wasn't all. His skin was a mid-brown colour. A colour which had been made familiar in recent years by the influx of immigrants from India and Pakistan. A colour the English man-in-the-street had come to associate with bus-conductors, because the numerous Indian and Pakistani bus-conductors were more in the public eye than the equally numerous factory workers from those same countries.

Matthew frowned. He was nothing if not a snob, and his first thought was to wonder how a bus-conductor, of any colour, had gained entry to the exclusive Nirvana Club. His second thought was one of outrage that such an intruder had dared to accost him so familiarly.

But both these thoughts were banished by a third thought. Indian or Pakistani this fellow might be—but he was no bus-conductor. His diminutive height would have disqualified him for that job. His little legs wouldn't be able to cope with bus stairs in the rush hour.

So what was he? Something more appropriate to the social status expected of members of the Nirvana Club? Matthew conveniently forgot that his own social status derived from his relationship to Virgil Lodway and Dr. Timothy Lodway. That as a car salesman he would not have been rated very high in the Nirvana's social scale.

Maybe this midget was an Indian doctor or medical

student? There were swarms of them in British hospitals nowadays. Was his advice "Do not be so sad" a sample of his medical bedside manner to the despondent?

Matthew flushed with resentment. He'd had more than enough of medical men—and if this smiling little character thought . . .

Matthew said brusquely: "What the hell d'you mean?"

His angry eyes noticed that the midget was wearing no turban; that his black hair was trimmed in the Western style. And that his thin, aquiline nose and his cheeks were pock-marked.

Unabashed, the midget continued to grin. He climbed agilely on to a bar stool so that he was much nearer Matthew's level.

"I meant—do not be so sad!" he said blandly. His dark, poodle eyes met Matthew's furious glare with serene equanimity.

"Huh!" For the purpose of being offensive, Matthew reverted viciously to his first assumption about the midget's probable sphere in life. He said insultingly: "Is that what you say to the passengers waiting in the queue? 'Do not be so sad—there'll be another bus along some time!' "

The midget showed his white teeth in another unabashed grin.

"It's what I would say to the bus queue if I were a bus-conductor! But as I own an Indian restaurant, I say it to anyone who looks downcast! It is a habit!"

Matthew's mouth twisted unpleasantly. "That habit must make you very popular, uh? All it needs to cure anyone's troubles is for some grinning idiot to say 'Do not be so sad!' "

"Not idiot!" the midget objected, still grinning. "And what I said isn't always an empty form of words. Sometimes troubles can be cured. You'll have another drink?"

Matthew scowled.

"If that's your cure-all, let me tell you it doesn't work. I've tried it." His eyes narrowed. He said vaguely: "Anyway, I thought hard liquor was against you fellows' religion. . . ."

The midget's perpetual grin widened. "There is very little that is contrary to my . . . religion!"

For a couple of seconds that seemed interminable, the dark eyes held Matthew's gaze. It needed an effort of will for Lodway to force his glance away, and when he had done so he felt that he knew more about this undersized stranger than words could have expressed.

"Huh!" he grunted. "Okay—make it another scotch."

To the hovering barman the midget called a polite order. His own drink was a double whisky which he began to dispose of undiluted while Lodway was adding water to his.

"So . . . ?" Matthew invited unsmilingly.

The midget's black eyebrows rose half an inch.

"So . . . ?" Matthew repeated. "You've landed yourself here, drinking with me. But why? Why me?"

"I told you. You looked so sad——"

"And now I'm supposed to be happy? Sorry to disappoint you——"

"You have much on your mind. Black thoughts." The dark eyes were scanning Matthew's scowling face. "You are filled with . . . hatred . . . !"

Matthew gave a soft laugh.

"So you're a mind-reader, eh? What Hollywood would call 'The Littlest Seer!' "

The midget joined in the laugh.

"Hollywood might!" he agreed. "But at my *ashram* I was called Swami Barham Lal Sivasan!"

Matthew blurted: "Swami! So you're another fortune-teller and you want to read my——" He stopped abruptly. He no longer had a palm for anyone to read.

Mildly the midget said: "Fortune-teller? No, I'm not a fortune-teller——"

"A fakir!" Matthew said impatiently. "Don't tell me you lie on beds of nails and do the Indian rope trick!"

"I could do both—if they were worthy of my . . . talents——"

"Your talents," Matthew suggested, "running more to making curry in your Indian restaurant!"

For a fleeting instant the midget's grin vanished and in his eyes there was a menacing blow which caused Matthew an uneasy thrill. To conciliate the midget he quickly followed up with a semi-humorous but more flattering suggestion.

"Or you're one of these holy men——"

The suggestion immediately restored the midget's humour. Again he did not answer in words, but his face split in a wide grin that was quite unholy. Lodway's latest suggestion had caused a deep sardonic amusement.

Annoyed, Matthew said: "Or you're going to try to sell me a lucky charm so that I won't be so sad——"

The amused eyes crinkled. "Lucky—or unlucky!"

"What d'you mean?"

The little man drained his drink.

"Your face just now was filled with . . . hatred. Unfulfilled hatred. For that the cure is an unlucky 'charm.' Unlucky for the person you hate!"

Matthew scoffed. "Charm! I thought it was something like that. Powerful Eastern amulet—made in Birmingham!"

Swami Barham Lal Sivasan shook his head.

"What I referred to would be made in Stilford! But it would not be anything to wear . . . anything made of metal. I was referring to the power of——" He bit off what he had been about to say.

And that intrigued Matthew more than what the man had actually said.

Matthew laughed again, but a little less derisively.

"Oh—you mean spells! Curses!"

That smile remained infuriatingly bland. "Do I? Whatever I mean, it can't be discussed here. But if you've the courage of your . . . maledictions, and would care to come with me . . ."

"Why not?" The implied doubt of his courage decided Lodway at once. He finished his scotch-and-water. "Where?"

"Would you prefer to go in my car or your own?"

"I'll follow yours, so's I can drive home afterwards. But what you have to say had better be interesting!"

To that the swami didn't bother to reply.

Matthew was impressed by the nearly-new Humber Super Snipe that the midget drove out of the Nirvana car park a couple of minutes later, and which he guessed must have been fitted with a special seat and foot controls for its diminutive driver.

Since his mutilating operation Matthew had exchanged his Austin Healey for an automatic Zephyr, with which his artificial hands could cope. In this he followed the Humber across town to a shabby-genteel district that was in slow decay. Surprisingly, it was here that the midget had his Indian Restaurant, named the Shalimar.

Optimistically, the restaurant was open, but the man who claimed to own it drove the Humber into a yard at the rear, where there was ample room for Lodway to park his Zephyr too.

As Lodway climbed out, he saw that his host was already walking to one of the two rear doors of the building and beckoning him to follow.

Unlocking the door, the swami led the way inside. Relocking the door behind them, he said: "The other rear door is for the restaurant kitchen. This door is for my separate private quarters, and only I have a key to it."

Matthew could well believe it. After the seediness of the surrounding neighbourhood and the restaurant frontage, he was astonished by the splendour already apparent in here.

Even the softly-lighted passage along which they were walking was fitted with a luxuriously thick and richly-coloured carpet which absorbed all sound of their footsteps. And the room into which he was next conducted was opulent, exotic, sybaritic in its brilliant luxury.

A room of Asiatic magnificence. Carpet of an even deeper, softer pile, strewn with a colour-spectrum of rugs. Chased-silver lamps, bronze-and-enamel trays, ebony cabinets inlaid with gold. A low ottoman with silk-covered cushions.

On the walls, tapestries of intricate design. Between them, framed works of art. Most of them being small pictures in the flat, stylised technique of Indian primitives. But a large gilt frame was occupied by a representational oil painting of a scene he recognised. The erotic paradise promised to the faithful by Islam's Prophet, with lounging turbaned men being ministered to by alluring, half-naked young houris.

Seeing the direction of his appreciative gaze, his host murmured the quatrain from the Koran which had inspired the painting:

> Verily for the pious is a blissful abode, Gardens and vineyards, Damsels with swelling breasts of suitable age, And a brimming cup. . . .

"You're a Moslem?" Lodway asked, turning towards him.

Smiling sardonically, the Indian said: "Obviously not, considering what I have offered you! That scene just happens to appeal to me. Neither am I a Hindu. I am a swami of that dark religion which has no name."

His glance was momentarily diverted towards two hideous heads in *bas-relief*, hung between tapestries. The glowering faces reminded Lodway of gargoyles.

"What are they?" he asked, frowning with distaste.

"*Assuras!* What you would call demons."

"I've seen prettier things!" Lodway commented laconically.

"You are just about to see something prettier. Even we not-so-pious can have our little paradise—here and now!"

The midget pressed an ivory button set in the wall within easy reach from the ottoman. In an adjoining room a bell could be heard to give a soft tinkle.

After a half-minute of silence, the inlaid further door swung soundlessly open.

6:
Emergency Call

INTO THE ORNATE room glided an Indian girl of remarkable grace and beauty.

She was dressed in a style similar to that of the attendant houris in the painted conception of the Prophet's paradise.

Sandalled feet with red-lacquered toenails. A sari of fine green silk which clung to her calves and thighs as she walked and sheathed her hips and waist with glistening emphasis. From a little above the waist the sari narrowed to pass over one shoulder, leaving entirely bare the other shoulder and both exquisitely modelled breasts.

The restaurant owner said to Lodway: "As well as being what you think, she is also a *chela*—a disciple—of mine."

Almost mesmerised by this domiciliary jewel in what was so depressed an area of the town, Lodway nodded dumbly.

"Sit down!" his host invited, indicating one of the three armchairs in the room. "You'll have another drink?"

His eyes following the girl, Matthew muttered: "Uh—yes! Certainly!"

After a glance at the midget, the girl glided across to a low, circular bronze table. On it stood several cut-glass goblets and a long-necked bottle made of some decorated ceramic. Apparently only one kind of drink was being offered, because the girl poured from the one bottle into two of the glasses, without asking questions.

When she approached Lodway with one of the glasses, which contained a small measure of a straw-coloured liquid, his eyes absorbed every detail of her appearance. The slender hands with their pointed red nails. The wide bangles on the flexible wrists. The raven sheen of the smooth blue-black hair, parted in the middle. The caste mark in the centre of her forehead. The large dark eyes beneath the painted eyebrows. The moist red lips. The twin promontories of femininity. . . .

He passed his tongue from one side of his mouth to the other and put out his gloved hands for the proffered glass. His emotional excitement made him even more awkward with the artificial hands than usual. He managed to grasp the glass but caused some of its contents to splash over the rim. Tears of humiliation stung his eyes at his clumsiness under the gaze of this girl he would have liked to impress. Mentally he cursed the two people responsible for his oafish inadequacy.

The midget had lighted a cigarette and now offered his case to Lodway. Lodway had helped himself to a cigarette by the time the girl came back with a glass for the little restaurateur. When he had taken it from her, she glided out of the room—without having uttered a word. The door closed on her.

"Don't worry," the midget said to Lodway, with cynical consolation for his obvious disappointment. "She wouldn't have been for you anyway!" He was studying his guest keenly. "But—I think we are now ready to resume our conversation?"

Lodway nodded indifferently.

Facing him from his seat on the edge of the ottoman, the Indian said: "I see hatred in your eyes. . . . I sense it radiating from the internal fire that is consuming you. Unless you expel that fire by expressing your hatred, its inward flames will reduce your life to ashes!"

"All right!" Matthew turned to him decisively. "If you want to know, I hate two people who . . . robbed me. Robbed me of something beyond price. Something I can't recover. And there's nothing I can do about it."

"That is where you are wrong!" the self-styled swami contradicted. "There is something you can do. You may not be able to rectify the wrong, but you Westerners have a saying: 'Revenge is sweet.' It is a true saying. When there is nothing else to console a man who has been wronged, revenge is a very sweet-smelling and soothing balm!"

"I've told you!" Lodway scowled impatiently. "There's nothing I can do—even in the way of revenge. Nothing. They—they've guarded themselves against revenge. If anything . . . happened to either of them, I would immediately be suspect. There's nothing I can do."

"You're wrong!" The midget leaned forward. "You're wrong because you think of revenge in a crude way. Of harming them by physical violence or physical poison. But there are other, more subtle, methods——"

"Oh, yes! We got to that in the club, didn't we! Spells, curses! Is that what you're suggesting? Mumbo-jumbo and incantations? I suppose you think there'd be money in it for you—but if you imagine I'm going to pay you to put on an act and——"

"Stop!" the Indian said gently. "Again you're thinking in material terms. You immediately assume that I would want cash for giving you the revenge you want. Well—I leave that to depend on results. If future events give you reason to be grateful to me, you can make a voluntary financial token of appreciation."

Lodway gave a sceptical grin.

"Not payment in advance? Then either you're a super optimist or you've no use for money!"

"I have a use for money—but in this matter money isn't my only motive. There are other satisfactions than financial reward. Have you never heard of people doing good for its own sake? Then why not the converse? I think that, crude as you are, you and I are fundamentally two of a kind——"

His glance flickered momentarily towards one of the *bas-relief* demons on the wall.

"That," he said, "I sensed in the club, from your psychic vibrations. It is why I approached you."

Lodway shrugged wearily.

"All right. Even if what you're saying is all moonshine, what harm can it do me? If you fail to do what you're hinting at, I'll owe you nothing. And, of course, you will fail."

He suddenly remembered that the cigarette he was holding was not yet ignited. It was thinner than English cigarettes and its paper cylinder was of a pale brown colour. Some Indian product. He raised it to his mouth and looked about for a lighter.

The midget lifted a heavy brass lighter from a low tabourette and held its flame to the tip of Lodway's cigarette.

From the first shallow puffs before the tobacco was fully ignited . . . no sensation. But then——! Lodway inhaled deeply.

The smoke was acrid. It smelt like a smouldering piece of coarse old rope. His first reaction to the smoke was a feeling of suffocation. Then his heart began to hammer forcefully. His vision went abruptly out of focus.

The palpitations eased, but he was left dizzy. He narrowed his eyes till his vision was no longer blurred, and stared at the midget.

"What is it?" he asked slowly, gesturing with the cigarette.

Again that grin. "Haven't you guessed? It's Indian hemp. What we call hashish and you would call marijuana. One cigarette won't harm you, and it's not one of the drugs of addiction."

"Isn't it? Then why do people keep smoking it?"

"Because it makes them feel happy. Try it, if you're not afraid."

Again Lodway responded to the slur on his courage. He returned the cigarette to his lips and drew on it again. One cigarette certainly couldn't hurt him, and he had the will-power to refuse another.

This time his heart again beat forcefully and rapidly, but he did have a surprising feeling of elation. An inclination to laugh. So it *was* all right. Paying no further attention to the cigarette, he looked at his host again and went on smoking automatically, as he would have done with any ordinary cigarette.

"We were saying . . ." the midget murmured. "If nothing happens you will owe me nothing. But if I succeed you will pay me two hundred pounds."

In his new mood of careless euphoria, Matthew nodded indifferently.

"All right. So—begin! Let me see you mix your potions and make your incantations or whatever it is you do!"

Swami Barham Lal Sivanson slowly shook his head.

"No. The things that are done I do in privacy. They are not for . . . squeamish Western stomachs. But it is the result that matters . . ."

He stopped, because Lodway was no longer listening.

After half-a-dozen inhalations of the hemp, Lodway was feeling the effects. His head was dizzy but felt curiously light. It felt as though it were being stretched upward. And he was sweating.

Sweating—and intermittently shivering. And his legs now felt remote and uncontrolled. His vision was again blurred.

But it was his thoughts which were most affected. They were almost delirious. Staring straight ahead, he could see that picture of Islam's paradise. But now he didn't see the frame. He saw the scene as though it were some three-dimensional celestial reality, supported and surrounded by drifting clouds.

The figures depicted in it were not only three-dimensional. They were moving! One of the voluptuous houris turned to look straight at him—and her face was the face of the living girl who had served him with his drink.

Living? *Had* that girl been living? Been real? Or had she been only a figment of his imagination, inspired by the sight of those much more realistic figures now moving about in that scene among the clouds?

Whether or not she had actually served him with a drink, she was real enough in that exotic scene before him now. And the sight of her was giving him urgent, hungry thoughts.

He wanted to climb up there into that cloud-girt scene and join in the revelry which was now taking place. He wanted tactile confirmation that the girl really was three-dimensional, living, warm, sensate. . . .

He stumbled awkwardly up on to his feet, swaying. The room in which he was standing tilted giddily. His knees were hinging under him, unable to support the weight of his lengthening body.

He dropped the cigarette and reached out towards that maddeningly enticing houri with the face he recognised. He was sweating profusely. But he was happy. Happy with hungry but confident anticipation of the ecstatic bliss he was about to grasp in that wonderland just ahead of him.

He heard the midget laughing—and joined in the laughter. That talk of spells and curses . . . it was all a joke, of course. A tremendous, excruciating joke, just between the two of them. Between himself and that tiny swami.

Nothing would, or could, come of it. But it was fun to pretend that it was serious and genuine and that something sinister would happen. Fun to laugh at its seriousness while pretending to believe it. . . .

He lurched forward, off-balance. And that seductive houri he hungered for was smiling directly at him and beckoning him on.

He tried to take another step forward. But his long, long legs simply liquefied and collapsed under him.

Like a cinematic "dissolve," the painted scene shrank and faded . . . dwindling and receding into an incredible distance.

But his blurring gaze could not follow it. Because he was bodily plunging down . . . down . . . down . . . into a pit packed with suffocating, black and blinding wool.

And as he sank helplessly into its soporific embrace, he still heard the laughter of the Indian midget . . . mingled with his own muffled, hysterical laughter.

They were the last sounds of which he was conscious before oblivion closed over him.

When Matthew Lodway next opened his eyes he was lying in a hunched attitude on the rear seat of his car.

And the car was in a municipal free car park a quarter of a mile away from the district into which he had followed the owner of the Indian restaurant.

Yellow light from distant street lamps dissipated some of the gloom inside the car. Lodway eased himself round on the seat, got his feet to the floor and peered painfully out through a side window.

Painfully, because the blood circulation was pounding

in his head with vicious power and remorseless monotony. And he felt sick.

He looked at the luminous dial of his wrist-watch—and was astounded. It was less than an hour since he had left the Nirvana Club. Yet, by his mental clock, days seemed to have passed. Had they?

Apparently not, because he didn't feel hungry.

But the act of leaving the Nirvana Club now seemed distant in time and remote in unreality.

Had he really left the club with an Indian midget? Had he actually gone to an Indian restaurant, met a half-naked Indian girl—and experienced that weird craving to enter the world of the painted picture?

Or had it all been a phantasm, a mental illusion?

But—the Indian hemp he had smoked? He felt as though under the influence of some drug he had never before sampled. Had he in fact smoked a reefer—but one given him not by an Indian midget but by someone else? Some marijuana peddler he had forgotten? And was the Indian midget merely part of his drug-inspired fantasy? A drug-distorted version of the actual peddler?

He grunted. His stomach heaved in nauseous protest against an abuse of his body chemistry. His nerves felt taut, his muscles strung-up to an unendurable tension.

Having lived in a medical environment all his life, he knew that what he needed, and needed badly, was a sedative. And in his flat he had some pheno-barbitone tablets. The few remaining of the supply he'd been given when the stumps of his amputations had been causing him sleepless nights.

He wasn't fit to drive, but for him driving when unfit was no new experience. Besides, the distance to his flat was only a short one. Not like it would have been had he still been living in the house out at Crestleigh.

The Indian midget, if he actually existed, had chosen a discreet way of getting rid of him. Having him carried out to the Zephyr and driven to this car park.

Had the Indian searched his guest's pockets while that guest had been unconscious? Lodway tapped his breast pocket. His wallet was still in it. Had its contents been examined they would have told the snooper very little. Lodway's pockets contained nothing to identify him.

A man of his tastes and habits didn't always want to be identifiable. He had passed out, from alcoholic over-indulgence, in some very peculiar places and circumstances. And while going under names other than his own. It had become an habitual precaution, on a night out, to carry nothing by which he could be identified. One never knew what opportunities might crop up . . . or what the repercussions might be.

So all the Indian had—if there was an Indian—was the number of Lodway's car. And that wouldn't be of much interest to him unless he should see the car again. Mightn't be a bad idea to trade it in for another model.

Racked with nausea, Lodway got out of the back of the car, staggered to the front offside door and climbed in behind the steering wheel. Ha!—the key was still in the ignition!

At this time of night traffic was thin. By sheer good luck Lodway reached his address without mishap. He even managed to drive the car into the garage with no worse damage than a scraping of its nearside front bumper.

Getting up to the flat was the most difficult part. By now his nerves were almost at screaming pitch and his eyes felt as though they were burning.

With his legs and arms shaking, he reached his bedroom and found the little brown bottle containing the tablets. In the bathroom he drew a glass of water and washed a couple of the tablets down his dry throat.

Till the tablets should take effect—if they were going to—he would be too keyed-up to sleep. But he stumbled back into the bedroom and flung himself, fully-dressed, on to his bed.

In half-an-hour there was a miraculous difference. The pounding in his head had stopped. The nausea had gone. His nerves were no longer like taut wires. The appropriate treatment had necessarily been a sedative of some kind, but evidently pheno-barbitone had been just the right antidote to that damned marijuana.

Relaxed, he drowsily closed his eyes. Ten minutes later, still fully-dressed, he was serenely asleep.

Next morning he went to work as usual. But while sitting at his desk he was wondering about the events—or the hallucinations—of the previous night.

It would be fairly easy to find out of the registered membership of the Nirvana Club included an Indian midget. Though it was quite possible that the midget had been only a guest of a member.

It would be even easier to find out if that Indian taurant actually existed and if it was owned by a midget. But—to what purpose?

If there really should be anything in what the fellow had said about revenging the wrong to his guest—good luck to him. If it had all been a huge joke—all right, it was best left at that.

But at mid-day a sardonic thought struck Matthew Lodway.

That what the swami had promised could be anything more than a joke seemed very unlikely indeed. But in case—just in case—of the remote possibility of something sinister behind it, it might be a wise thing for Matthew to drive out to the Lodway house this evening.

If any malefic prospects hung over Timothy or their father, it was advisable to get another cheque from one or the other of them while it was still possible. Matthew's mouth twisted. He had told the swami that sudden death for either of them would be dangerous for himself. But there was no guarantee that any other kind of calamity called down on them would leave them able to supply further cheques!

Matthew gave a mirthless grin. It was about time for another cheque anyway! He was a big spender.

So just after eight in the evening, he drove the automatic Zephyr out to Crestleigh and up the well-remembered drive to the house.

And while he was still a dozen yards from the house, Matthew emitted a soft hiss of pleased surprise. At the side of the house was parked a mini-car he recognised.

Alison's . . . !

He parked his own car beside hers. There was no other car in sight He looked into the garage. No cars there, either. So both his father and Timothy were out.

And, at nearly eight-thirty, the cook and the handyman would have gone home!

Matthew's heart was thumping fast as he went through the open front door into the house. Thumping now with the excitement of a pleasurable anticipation.

He crossed the hall, pushed open the lounge door. And there she was. Alone in the summer dusk, with no lights switched on.

Alison Garfield, who had been the fiancée of his late brother, Alan. Alison, cause of the corrosive jealousy which had made him murder Alan.

Alison, waiting here on the settee for Timothy or his father to arrive.

As if suddenly aware of Matthew's intent stare, she jerked out of her reverie and looked up. She saw Matthew standing at the doorway.

"Oh, hullo!" she said awkwardly, but with a fair pretence of cordiality. Then, to explain why she was alone in the house: "Timothy was here when I arrived, but he had to go out on an emergency call soon after. So he told me to wait. He'll be back."

"And father?" Moving idly into the room, Matthew made the question sound casual.

"Oh—he's out at some university conference. . . ."

Matthew stopped, reached back an arm and closed the

door behind him. Now, slowly, he moved directly towards Alison. And, even in the dusk, something in his expression disturbed her.

Jerkily she said: "But Timothy will be back soon. . . ."

Matthew's teeth gleamed in a stark grin.

All the hungers of the previous evening were ravaging him again. And always they centred on Alison.

That elfin-faced kid he'd followed to the amusement arcade had been a substitute for Alison. Even last night's Indian girl—if she existed—had been only a substitute for Alison. All the women there'd ever been in his life had only been substitutes, since he'd met Alison.

He remembered that scene in the summer-house when she'd been with Alan. And jealousy fanned the heat of his hunger to an unbearable flame.

Here was Alison herself—no substitute. Alison, alone with him for the first time in a year.

He continued moving slowly towards her.

"Soon?" he smiled. "If it's an emergency, how can you be sure he'll be back soon?" His smile widened. His breathing was audible. "Anyway, there'll be time. . . ."

Now he was only a yard away from where she huddled back against an arm of the settee. Cornered, she watched his purposeful approach. There was no mistaking the seriousness of his intention.

Her instinctive distrust of him, which had only been lulled by his out-of-character concern for a youngster in danger, was now fully awakened—and needed no further justification.

Her eyes were wide and their pupils followed the menacing movements of his black-gloved hands.

She saw those hands, with a horrifying unnatural rigidity, reach down for her.

7:
In Confidence

ALISON TRIED to evade the hands, but one of them pinned her by a shoulder, forcing the shoulder-blade flat against the arm of the settee. She struggled to break free.

"How dare you!" she gasped, clinging to a flimsy hope of stopping him before he should commit himself to going any further. "If this is a joke——"

Even to her, it was that suggestion itself which had a grim humour. Matthew's grin became gaunt, impatient.

"Be your age, Alison! I'm going to stop you moping over Alan. You must have noticed my close resemblance to him——"

"Only physical!" she flung at him contemptuously.

His grin widened. "That's quite enough. It's the physical aspect I'm thinking of! Who better to stop you brooding over Alan—than a brother who's practically his double!"

Panting, she stared up at him without answering, gathering her strength to renew the struggle.

His other hand came down on her left shoulder . . . hard, inhuman, frightening.

But the horror in her eyes was not wholly—nor even

mainly—due to the artificiality of the hands pinning her down. It was chiefly due to the revival of the sinister impact he had always made on her before his accident. The hands horrified her because they were his, because even artificial hands had an evil use at the service of his evil personality.

His present forcible attention and obvious immediate purpose would in themselves constitute a criminal offence. But now that she had lost the last shred of the illusion created by the circumstances of his accident, she sensed with a terrifying certainty that even that purpose represented only a fraction of his ruthless capabilities.

The same kind of advances could have been made by another man and have represented an ungovernable but fundamentally affectionate passion. But Matthew Lodway's evident relish of her fear hinted at a basic sadism which had prompted this attack and would direct its course.

In the next few seconds the attack was launched—in a way which her musical knowledge made her weirdly aware had become almost traditional in a dozen passionate operas.

The grip on the collar of her summer blouse. The rip of the thin material . . . the hot glare in his eyes at sight of the bare shoulder and inadequate bra.

And so far, as she was also weirdly aware, he himself had not actually touched her. All that had yet touched her was the material of his black gloves on those factory-made hands!

The thought spurred her into action. With his heated face just above her, she exerted the full power of her gathered strength.

Her greatest difficulty was in dislodging his weight. But when she had managed to squirm free of it and his hands sought a digital grip of her flesh—she received a welcome surprise.

Instinctively she grabbed at his hands to force them

away from her. Instinctively she twisted them. Her success was immediate. With their strength boosted by fear, her hands were more powerful than the grip he could exert with those artificial fingers and thumbs. The twist she gave his hands was stronger than his power of resistance!

Instantly he realised the same fact. From his working mouth came a low snarl of rage. Into his hot eyes came tears of maddening frustration. He had been able to pin her down with his artificial hands—but he couldn't exert a grip with them that could hold her still now she was no longer pinned.

He tried for another grip—and the attempt was futile. She was away and darting breathlessly to the door.

She had it open and was through before he had scrambled to his feet. Before he had reached the hall he heard the whirr of her car starter. When he got to the front door the mini-car was already speeding down the drive.

He stood at the doorway, shaking with fury and snuffling with self-pity. The time, he realised, was now past when he could induce unwilling females to see reason. From hereon he would be restricted to the willing. Which meant the mercenary and promiscuous. It would be like a collector of first editions finding himself condemned to rely on the circulating libraries.

But—the more immediate question. Would Alison tell Tim or the old man?

Matthew decided not to wait for a cheque. If Tim should find him here and Alison gone, he might get nasty ideas even if Alison should say nothing.

Conversely, if she did make a song-and-dance about it, but there was no evidence that he'd been here this evening, he could deny the accusation. He could say she was still distraught from the loss of Alan and that her accusation was the kind of wishful-thinking fantasy often dreamed up by frustrated women. That would shake her!

The old man and Tim could think what they chose, but in the absence of proof . . .

Matthew slammed the front door after him, to make it look as though Alison had left in a perfectly composed way and had her aberration later. He drove out of the grounds and back to Stilford. To avoid any chance of meeting Tim on the way, he took a long detour back to the town.

But even the succession of scotches he sank when back in his flat did nothing to soften the harsh outline of his future.

It was not only Alison who could say "no" to him now.

Timothy Lodway frowned in surprise when he reached home and found the house deserted. Alison had evidently remembered to lock the door on leaving—but why had she left so soon? His emergency call hadn't taken very long.

Perhaps she had a headache or something. Anyway, he obviously had to phone her to apologise for having wasted her visit.

She was at home when he rang her flat. And her voice sounded unusually agitated.

"Sorry for dashing away like that, Alison," he said. "Feel pretty badly about wasting your evening. You're feeling all right, I hope?"

In a voice which, even on the phone, sounded ragged and subdued, she said: "I'm all right now, Timothy. But there's something you ought to know about—because I shan't be coming to the house again."

"What?" He was quite astonished. "Alison—I know I treated you shabbily this evening, rushing off. But surely you understand what a doctor's life's like! If it had been tomorrow evening it would have been all right, because I shan't be on call then——"

"It's not that, Timothy. I realise you weren't to blame for leaving me. But—look! I can't discuss it on the phone——"

His puzzled and worried frown deepened. "Sounds serious! Haven't offended you in any other way, have I? Listen. As I told you, I shall have a free evening tomorrow. Meet me in town and we'll have dinner——"

"It's hardly the sort of thing I could discuss over a restaurant meal——"

"Mmm—does sound as if I'm in the dog-house! All right, if the weather holds we'll go for a little run in the car and you can tell me all about it."

"Very well. Pick me up at my flat. About seven-thirty?"

"Seven-thirty it is. And please believe I'm sorry for this evening, Alison."

"Good-night, Timothy."

She still sounded coldly formal. At least one member of the Lodway family was evidently in her bad books.

Timothy shrugged ruefully, and went to the kitchen to find himself a cold meal.

In case Matthew should dare to come to her flat, Alison kept its front door locked all the time she was at home during the following twenty-one hours.

She was ready and waiting for Timothy when he called for her next evening. Before unlocking the door to him she made sure of his identity.

She was looking pretty, as usual, but her face was pale and serious. It brought a frown back to his brow. She'd said she understood the exigencies of his profession, but if it wasn't his abrupt departure last evening that had upset her—what on earth was it?

She gave no hint even when seated beside him in the car.

"You've eaten?" he asked politely.

"Yes." Again her manner was remote. What she was going to tell him promised to be very unpleasant.

"Then shall we go along the river?" he suggested.

"Yes—just the place. I . . . what I have to say needs privacy."

His brows slanted. Shrugging, he started off and drove through town as quickly as the evening traffic would allow.

The outer suburbs fell away behind them and he took the branch road that ran parallel with the river. A picturesque road with wooded hills climbing away to the left and with tree branches casting their shadows on the grass verge.

"Pleasant evening!" Timothy said. The river was glistening in the reflected light reaching its calm surface from the evening sun, itself now obscured by the woods.

"Er—yes," she said, without appreciation.

They passed a few schoolboy cyclists and a pony rider—then reached regions beyond the energies of those muscular means of transport.

Timothy slowed and glanced at Alison. They were now in the country. This, at least, should be private enough for her.

"This do?" he asked.

She nodded.

He steered in till they were on the grass verge and in the shade of thickly foliaged tree branches. He braked, cut the engine and exhaled a long breath.

Relaxing in his seat, he half-turned so that he could see her face properly.

She was still pale and solemn.

"Now, Alison," he invited gently. "Tell me all about it. How have I offended you?"

Mollified by his professional manner, she tried to smile—but he was surprised to see sudden tears in her eyes.

"It isn't you, Tim," she blurted, her self-control cracking. "It's—it's Matthew——!"

As if afraid to draw back now that she had broken the ice, she plunged into a rapid account of Matthew's attack on her the previous evening.

She did not mention that her indignation was that of a woman who claimed the right to choose her own lover and who had a particular antipathy to Matthew. Omitting any hint of her intimate relations with Alan, which she supposed to be unknown to anyone else, she gave the impression that her indignation came from an entirely virginal sense of outrage, which would have been aroused by advances from any man at all.

"I don't want to make a fuss, Timothy," she finished. "Don't even mention it to your father or Matthew. But you do see why I can't come to the house again. If Matthew should happen to be there . . . I simply couldn't face him. . . ."

She frowned resentfully. "What kind of girl does he think I am, Tim? How could he do it? How could he?"

One of Timothy's hands came over to rest soothingly on her shoulder. But his reply shocked her.

"Obviously he couldn't!" Tim said with brutal indifference. "He bungled it."

Her eyes stared into his in utter disbelief. In his face was an expression of equal disbelief—as though Timothy himself was amazed and shocked by what he had just said.

She forced a nervous smile to her lips.

"That—that's hardly a nice way of putting it!" Her voice had become a little husky.

She searched his face again, for reassurance.

But his shocked look had faded. In its place was dawning a slow grin, totally unlike any expression she had seen on Tim's face before. A cynical grin horribly reminiscent of Matthew's.

For the first time this evening, for the first time in Tim's company, a spasm of positive fear stabbed through her.

But Tim . . . it couldn't be . . .

His voice broke in on her bewildered thoughts. Crudely, callously—with no resemblance to Tim's usual professional suavity.

"Matthew bungled it," he said coarsely. "But I can certainly understand him trying!"

His hands moved slowly along her shoulder, towards her throat.

Its movement intensified her nervousness—but it also banished Tim's grin. Again there showed in his face an expression of shocked surprise.

It was as if he couldn't credit what his hand was doing. As if its action amazed and horrified him.

But his hand wasn't deterred. And not only did it continue its slow menacing movement, but his other hand moved up and came to rest on her other shoulder.

Her face, already pale, blenched to a pallor that was almost corpse-like.

"Tim . . . !" she faltered. "Is this some joke?"

Her features twitched to the instant recollection that she had asked Matthew the same question. And now—as then—the question mocked her with its hollowness.

The two hands on her shoulders converged towards her throat.

Tim's face, now looming above hers, was no longer looking shocked. It was looking hungry . . . and purposeful . . . and pitiless.

She tried to utter a brave, indignant protest. But Timothy's right hand fastened on her throat and compressed it to silence. Her neck was forced back over the squab of the seat—just as Matthew had forced her back over the arm of the settee.

But the evil glare radiating from Tim's menacing eyes told her that, even if she could have uttered a sound, pleading would be wasted. That it would be like beating futile fists against the closing door of her doom.

It was not just because of the violence he had already used—had used from the outset. Even if she were prepared to explain away the bruises on her throat and he could be absolutely sure that she would make no complaint to the Law, it would make no difference, she realised.

His eyes again had the look she had seen in Matthew's. It told her beyond doubt that what he had already done, and his obvious immediate intention, did not represent the full extent of his capabilities and purpose.

It was no simple, uncomplicated appetite that had motivated Matthew's assault on her—and it was no simple, uncomplicated appetite that was now driving Timothy to the ultimate ruthlessness.

His hands tightened viciously on her throat. Hands of capable flesh-and-blood, reinforced with the muscular power of the forearms. Her senses swam into terror-hastened vertigo.

Methodically the hands continued their merciless programme. Alison's limp body was carried from the car and up the grassy incline into the woods.

She regained her senses to wince from the pain of her bruised throat, to shiver at the touch of cool evening air on uncovered skin. Her shivers became an ague when she saw his face, at close range, glaring down at her. He had no need to stifle her voice again while it was happening. She was incapable of any sound but a whispered croak.

. . . Till it was over—and the central terrifying thought sent hoarse words bursting frantically out of her dry throat.

"I won't tell anyone!" she babbled. "I won't make a fuss——!"

He grinned. "You made a fuss about Matthew—and he only tried!"

"But not about Alan! You know now you weren't the first. But there's something about Matthew——" Her babble was hysterical. "I won't tell anyone about *you*.

You needn't worry about your reputation . . . your career——"

His grin was devilish. "I won't!"

Again his two hands closed on her throat. For long minutes she suffered indescribably—knowing the horrors of a sadistic hell.

When he eventually drew away from her, she was dead.

He lifted her, carried her further into the gloomy depths of the wood.

Among tall weeds and grass he casually dumped her body. A moss-covered stone among the undergrowth caught his eye. When he had finished using it, her face and head were unrecognisable.

On reaching the brighter light of the roadside, he stood beside the car and raised his hands to study them.

Inevitably, the original operation had left scars encircling the wrists. Particularly noticeable because of the hairlessness of the scar tissue. But his father had got rid of those dangerous mementoes by means of delicate skin-grafts utilising hairy skin taken from the patient's thigh.

Fingers splayed, Timothy looked at his substitute hands in fascination, wondering at their macabre efficiency.

But while driving back to Stilford he was suddenly assailed by a nerve-storm which compelled him to stop the car.

Shaking uncontrollably, with tears dampening his face, he rested his head on the steering-wheel, appalled and overwhelmed by the infamy of what he had done this evening.

Could he really have committed such an atrocious crime? He—a respected, dedicated general medical practitioner?

He had a strange, frightening feeling of dual personality. As though part of his mind was looking back in dazed horror at what had given another part of his mind an evil satisfaction.

So this was the monstrous use he had made of his brother Matthew's hands!

When finding himself endowed with those substitute hands he had accepted the situation for three reasons. Because he could not denounce his father, since even Matthew wouldn't. Because Matthew accepted the situation without complaint. And because of the humanitarian, life-saving use he himself would be making of Matthew's hands.

Life-saving! What would his father say of the infamous use he had now made of them?

For several minutes, sick with self-revulsion and self-loathing, Timothy knew a strong temptation to rush to his father or the police—and confess the horrifying facts.

But he was no longer of one mind.

Before his tears were dry, his feeling of guilt gave way to considerations of personal safety. And again the dominance of his thoughts and feelings was gained by that part of his mind which remembered his crime with satisfaction.

And the horror was extinguished by the novel sense of gratification. A growing, saturating satisfaction—as though more than one avid appetite in his nature had been appropriately appeased.

For the time being. . . .

8: The Urge

DURING THE DAY following his attack on Alison, Matthew had waited in anticipation of an angry phone-call from his father or Timothy.

When there'd been none, he'd been relieved but surprised. Surprised because it had seemed certain that Alison would complain—if only because of the possibility of meeting him at the house again. That was something she wouldn't risk, and he couldn't quite magine her simply staying away in the future with no explanation to Timothy or the old man.

Besides, Timothy must have expected to find her in the house on his return, and some explanation of her absence would have been due.

But facts were facts. When a second day passed without a caustic phone-call about the matter, Matthew could only conclude that Alison had decided not to complain. Perhaps because she hadn't wanted to hurt the old man's feelings.

Then, on the evening of the second day after his attack on her, Matthew learned of another possible reason why she hadn't complained.

On the way home to his flat he bought a late edition of the local paper. And there it was, in the Stop Press column:

ORCHESTRA SECRETARY MISSING

Miss Alison Garfield, secretary of Stilford Philharmonic Orchestra, did not arrive for work today. Midday inquiries at her flat showed that the morning milk and paper were still outside her door. When there was no answer to repeated ringing, the door was opened with a pass-key and it was found her bed had not been slept in. Mr. Denis Kendrick, the orchestra manager, says she would have informed him of any emergency which might have called her away, so her absence is a mystery.

Matthew scowled over the report. Had he scared her worse than he'd realised? Frightened her into running away from the town without stopping to explain to anyone?

In that case there might still be a complaint to his father—through the post or by phone. With prompt effect on his cheques. Damn! Just when he'd thought she was letting the thing be forgotten, she had him in doubt again.

But wait a minute. She hadn't run away immediately. It was only on the second day after his attack on her that she hadn't gone to work. She'd been absent only for the second day.

Then what had happened? He might be in the clear after all, as she'd made no complaint on the first day. Perhaps her disappearance had nothing whatever to do with his assault on her. Maybe she had a new boyfriend she'd gone off with.

But it was queer she hadn't kept the orchestra informed of her movements.

Very queer indeed!

"Sorry to trouble you, gentlemen!"

Inspector Russell, of the Stilford C.I.D., had that impact of sheer physical bulk which made most policemen easily recognisable as such, and always would as long as physical dimensions were the primary recruiting criteria.

"Sit down, Inspector," Virgil Lodway invited. "Can I offer you a sherry?"

"Not on duty, thank you, sir."

But the inspector accepted a seat in the Lodway lounge and Timothy and his father waited to hear what he had to say.

"It's about Alison?" the surgeon suggested. "Alison Garfield?"

"Yes!"

"We saw the news item in the paper the other evening."

"Of course. She's been missing three more days since then. I understand the young lady had been engaged to one of your sons——"

"My late son, Alan. It was his death which ended the engagement. But Alison has kept in touch with us. Visits us quite frequently."

"When did you see her last, sir?"

The surgeon glanced at Timothy.

"How long, Timothy? About a fortnight, wasn't it?"

"About that," Timothy agreed.

That was her last visit known to his father. Timothy felt very glad that circumstances had prevented him telling his father of Alison's actual last visit to the house and of his meeting with her by arrangement on the following evening.

On the night of Alison's last visit there, Timothy had gone to bed before his father had returned from the university conference. And next morning he had gone out on an early call before his father had got up. Their respective jobs had then kept them apart for the rest of that day till the fatal evening.

So no one knew of his meeting with Alison that evening. And only one person knew of her visit to the house on the previous evening. Matthew!

In the circumstances, Matthew would be very unlikely to mention his knowledge of her visit.

Nobody—not even Matthew—knew that he, Timothy, had taken Alison out on the evening of her disappearance. There was nothing whatever to connect him with her disappearance.

But for a moment he had a vivid mental picture of her, lying in the woods as he had last seen her. And for an instant of weakness he had an impulse to shout his guilt. To surrender to justice this monster of depravity that he'd become.

Then the newer part of his personality regained its dominance and gave a cynical, silent chuckle.

He was a clever man. A professional man—not a crude crook with a criminal record. He was safe.

There were people disappearing every day. A few more would disappear before Alison's body would be found—by which time it might be decomposing.

Anyway, let them identify her body if they could. What he'd done to her with that stone had been more of a gesture than a real attempt to conceal her identity. A gesture adding to his destructive gratification.

There'd be plenty of suspects. A good-looking girl who'd worked with an all-male orchestra would have aroused plenty of jealousies and motives for murder.

He became aware that the inspector was talking again.

". . . Mr. Kendrick, the orchestra manager, is convinced she wouldn't have gone away voluntarily without letting him know why. But, unless there's been foul play, it seems she *has* gone away voluntarily. Could there be another man in her life now?"

Timothy said: "She hasn't mentioned one to us—but if there was one she might be a bit bashful about telling us, after all the affection she said she had for Alan. Still, she's young and attractive—and among all those men in the orchestra——"

The inspector broke in: "If she's gone away with a man, he isn't a member of the orchestra. None of them has been absent while she's been missing. It's a puzzle. She has no relatives in Stilford and she hasn't gone to her parents' home in Chester."

Timothy smiled. "Then perhaps she's found a new boy-friend outside the orchestra! So infatuated with him that she completely forgot to tell the orchestra manager they were going on a trip. She might even be staying with a sick girl-friend. It still seems a bit early to get alarmed."

"I agree!" Virgil Lodway said. "I daresay she'll be back in a day or two with some perfectly reasonable explanation."

"I hope so." The inspector stood up. "We have to make these inquiries, of course. Well—thank you both. I'll be getting along——"

Virgil Lodway escorted the policeman out to his car. Left alone, Timothy gave a long sigh of relief.

But he was also conscious of a feeling of exultation. Of a new contempt for the forces of law and order.

And, as if of their own volition, his homicidal hands twined together, in mutual congratulation and gloating.

In morning surgery next day, Timothy pressed the bell-button on his desk and waited for the next patient to come in.

It had been a great pleasure to come back to his old room and practice after his long absence. A pleasure to be back with his old partner, Dr. Dawson, now dealing with his own patients in an adjoining room.

On his return, even the most tiresome patients had seemed less tiresome than usual. His career was the most important thing in his life, and it was to these people that he was dedicated.

At this time of year the practice was not very busy and he would soon finish with the few patients now left in the waiting room.

A tap on his surgery door. The door opened. In came the next patient, Mrs. Matheson.

She was about thirty, dark-haired and shapely, with an attractive face.

He gave his usual smile of greeting and waved her towards the chair facing him.

"Well, Mrs. Matheson?" he prompted, when she was seated.

"It's my headaches, Doctor," she said. "They're as bad as ever. I really don't know how I stand them."

He gave a sympathetic frown. Her headaches were an old complaint. Privately he had always considered them neurotic in origin, a symptom of emotional frustration. But a suggestion of psychiatric treatment would have caused Mrs. Matheson a sense of outrage. What she wanted was to be regarded as a sufferer and to be given pain-relieving tablets or a bottle of "tonic."

"As bad as that, are they?" he murmured.

She passed a hand up under her dark hair, to caress the nape of her neck.

"The muscles here seem all knotted up," she said. "All tense. Sometimes I feel I could scream!"

He got up from behind his desk and came round to her. Walking behind her, he placed his hands at the nape of her neck where she had indicated.

"Here?" he asked.

"That's it, Doctor." Satisfied that she was receiving due attention, she closed her eyes, waiting for comforting massage.

His thumbs pressed against the hollow at the base of her skull and his fingers spread to either side of her neck. For a few seconds, thumbs and fingers explored the contours of her neck, seeking for abnormalities.

But he found none. He was about to take his hands

away—when suddenly he found himself ramming his thumbs deep into that hollow again and gripping the sides of her neck with the full force of his fingers.

She cried out in pain. Still he did not immediately release his grip. He did so only when she violently wrenched herself away. And even then his hands remained crooked and poised, as though robbed of prey.

"Doctor!" Mrs. Matheson was staring round at him in astonishment and anger. "You hurt me! Whatever were you doing?"

He came to himself with a jerk, as if emerging from a daze. He was asking himself the same question. Whatever had he been doing?

He mustered a smile and forced his hands down to his sides.

He muttered: "It—it was just to relieve the muscular cramp. As you may know, muscular cramp in the leg can be relieved by pricking the muscle with a needle. I—I was just trying a similar way of releasing the muscular tension in your neck!"

"Oh . . . !" She was frowning at him doubtfully, and raised her own hand to massage her neck.

Poor fool, he was thinking. If she only knew how close she had come to dying here in this surgery! Had her cry not brought him to his senses, those headaches of hers would have been cured for ever.

He walked back and reseated himself behind his desk.

"I'll write you a prescription, Mrs. Matheson," he said. "But try to relax. These headaches of yours are partly due to emotional tension. You must try to keep calm at all times."

Even, he was thinking sardonically, when your medical adviser is seized with a sudden overwhelming urge to take firm hold of your pretty and troublesome neck—and strangle you!

She went out smiling, as if satisfied with his impromptu explanation.

But when his last two patients had also gone, he sat hunched in his chair, badly frightened.

What was wrong with him? He had not come to terms with the fact of his murder of Alison Garfield—except for occasional moments when his conscience insisted on coming to the surface of his mind. And those moments were now becoming rarer.

But this impulse which had come to him this morning, right here in the surgery . . . Was he going mad?

What he had done to Alison had been quite separate from his professional life. And although the homicidal urge had come to him that night only when privacy had placed her at his mercy, it had not seemed to him an irrational impulse. Not an impulse beyond his control, had he wished to suppress it.

This morning's impulse, however, had undoubtedly been irrational. No rational urge would have caused him to endanger his professional career by attacking a patient in his own surgery. What had possessed him to do so?

It was only because Mrs. Matheson had cried out and broken away from his grip that she was still alive. That he knew. Had she delayed only another few seconds, till his grip on her neck had become secure, she would have died at his hands.

Once his hands had settled on her neck, it was as if his mind had become obsessed with one purpose. All other considerations had been excluded from his thoughts, and would have remained excluded—had she not violently wrenched herself free from that tightening grip.

Now those considerations he had excluded came rushing into his mind. His career . . . his personal safety. . . .

Strangely, he was not feeling particularly guilty about what he had done to his patient. He was glad she had come to no harm, but chiefly because any harm suffered by her in his surgery would have resulted in danger to himself.

And it was because of that danger that he had to control this new impulse of his. This urge to use his hands destructively instead of healingly. From now on he had to watch himself every minute—or a moment's impulse was going to bring his career crashing in ruin.

And his career still mattered to him, even though his sense of dedication to his patients' welfare seemed to be diminishing. For the sake of his career and reputation, he had to keep an iron control over all his irrational impulses.

Those impulses were just a phase. Soon the phase would be past. There would be no more homicidal urges . . . and the death of Alison Garfield would pass into oblivion.

Yes. The whole thing should be banished from his mind. What he wanted was distraction. He'd be free this evening. He'd see a film and have a drink afterwards. That would take him out of himself. . . .

The film at the Roxy Cinema was a good one. When Timothy came out of the vestibule and set off along the pavement in quest of a drink, he was in a tranquil mood.

His car was in the cinema car park, but he fancied a stroll around the streets before settling on a pub. Too much of his working day was spent in a car, making his rounds. A spot of fresh air and exercise was welcome.

He lit a cigarette and puffed it with enjoyment as he strolled along in the summer dusk.

The pub which eventually attracted him was The Rugged Staff. An old-fashioned pub with its entrance at the end of a narrow alley.

He made his way along the alley to the bright glazed double doors. For the next three-quarters of an hour he enjoyed the pub's bottled beer and the conviviality of its customers.

He was still in a tranquil mood when he came out into the alley again.

But the drunk he met half-way along the alley changed his mood—drastically.

The alley was gloomy, its only illumination being a lamp hung under its arch at the street end. The drunk was a tottering shadow trying to hold itself up against a side wall. As Timothy came along, the drunk reeled away from the wall and staggered into his path.

Timothy made to step round him, but the drunk again staggered into his path.

Timothy's tranquillity became disturbed.

"Let me get by!" he said curtly.

The drunk took offence.

"All ri', chummy—all ri'!" he said aggrievedly. "You —you don't own . . . the bloody alley . . . you know!"

He stood aside for Timothy to go by. But no sooner was Timothy level with him than the drunk lost his balance—and grabbed wildly for support. His arms clasped round Timothy's neck and his alcoholic breath wafted unpleasantly into Timothy's face.

Timothy's tranquillity vanished.

"Let go!" he said viciously, giving the fellow a push. But the push only made the drunk cling tighter.

"Take it easy, chummy!" he protested. "Jus' lemme . . . get my . . . bearings——"

He set his feet astride for security, and carefully removed his arms from Timothy's neck.

Then he vomited right down Timothy's chest.

The effect on Timothy was catastrophic. There was a drumming in his ears, a pumping of adrenalin into his bloodstream.

He gave a wordless snarl—and leapt at the staggering drunk.

As if by instinct, his hands found the drunk's thick neck.

Oblivious of his surroundings, of whether anyone else might be coming along the alley, he secured a stranglehold in the fleshy folds of the neck. His eyes glowed hot.

He continued to mouth wordless snarls. All his physical strength was forced along his rigid forearms into those throttling fingers and thumbs.

The drunk was choking obscenely. The stench of his vomit rose in a disgusting miasma.

But no one came along the alley to save him. His arms feebly flailed—in vain. His legs folded under him. Timothy stood over him, willing him to die.

And when his ruthless hands at last relaxed their grip and allowed the stranger to slump inert on the ground, Timothy knew that he had died.

He stepped clear of the body. Suddenly conscious of his own danger, he cast a nervous glance along the alley in each direction.

No sign of a third party!

With his own breath rasping in his throat, he stepped past the corpse and hurried along the alley to the street beyond.

On the pavement, the smell of his victim's vomit told him he could not go far unnoticed. Hurriedly he used his handkerchief to wipe off the worst of the mess, and he rammed the handkerchief into his pocket before continuing on his way.

He took a short cut back to the Roxy Cinema and its car park. It was only when he was driving the car out of town, home to Crestleigh, that he felt safe.

Safe for the moment—but again frightened.

Frightened because of a fact about himself which this second murder had taught him. That, in certain circumstances, he could *not* control his homicidal impulses!

It was by sheer chance, he knew, that no one had come into the alley while he had been committing murder. Sheer chance that there had been no eye-witness.

At the time of the killing he simply hadn't cared whether there was an eye-witness or not. All that had mattered had been to destroy that disgusting creature who had stood in his way and befouled him. Had instant execution been the penalty, he would still have killed the stranger then.

But what was the terrifying implication? That, if provoked, he was liable to make a murderous attack on anyone at any time—and in full view of witnesses!

He got into the Crestleigh house unseen. In his bedroom he quickly changed out of his soiled suit. When changed into a clean suit, he flung himself into a chair and stared desperately before him.

What could he do? He wasn't worried about the man he had killed. He was worried about his own future—the provocations that must lie ahead.

Again he looked at his hands. Two murders they had now committed for him.

In sheer fear of his own potentialities, he put his hands over his eyes—and sobbed.

9:
Psycho

"Oooh—innit creepy!"

Sandra James had been walking through the wood only a little over ten minutes, when she turned to her boyfriend Dave with a mock shudder.

Knowing what she wanted, he grinned and put an arm round her shoulder.

"That better?" he asked.

"Mmm—but don't get ideas, mind! No funny business."

"Your trouble's a suspicious mind, darlin'! Just relax. There's nothing in these woods can 'arm you——"

" 'Cept you!" she said, with a giggle.

" 'Cept me," he agreed. "But you know 'ow 'armless I am!"

"Yeh—in the daylight," she said. "But it's gettin' dark in these woods. Makes me feel a bit goosey——"

"Garn! We came 'ere for a bit o' dark, didn't we? Who you kiddin'?"

They continued to thread their way between the trees, their feet rustling through the undergrowth. The thick foliage overhead shut out most of the fading evening light. And in the intervals between their jocular remarks the pervading silence was eerie.

"Dave . . . !" Sandra's voice was low. "Don't you think we've come far enough? Let's turn back, Dave!" She peered up at his face, dim in the gloom.

"Turn back?" he protested. "Wivout what we've come for? 'Ave a 'eart, darlin'." He glanced about them. "Okay—this'll do. Take the weight off your feet, San'!"

With relief, she lowered herself to the ground, dry from the recent spell of fine weather. Eagerly Dave dropped down beside her. In another moment his mouth had fastened on hers and his hands were exploring.

Even while she had been walking the hem of her skirt had been three inches above her knees. In her present posture it had worked up a further three inches. The sheen of pale skin attracted Dave's interest. With her mouth temporarily released, Sandra relaxed, idly flinging an arm out alongside her.

Next moment she gavc a nervous yelp—and quickly lifted the limp arm. Immediately she emitted a little scream.

"Look, Dave! Oh, my God—look!"

He looked at the hand she had lifted, and stared in wonder. The hand looked as though it had suddenly erupted a crop of blackberries!

And then he saw that those "blackberries" were moving. Crawling! That they were actually a mass of flies.

"Sandra!" he blurted. "What——? Where——?"

Frantically she scrambled up on to her knees. Mutely she pointed that fly-covered hand in among the undergrowth that had been behind her.

"There, Dave! There——!" she whispered hoarsely.

Crouched beside her, he peered into the gloom-shrouded vegetation.

And then he felt sick.

Lying on its back among the tall undergrowth was

the body of a woman. And where her face should have been there was a seething mass of those "blackberries."

A colony of flies feasting on her congealed blood.

Wide-eyed with horror, Sandra jumped to her feet and frantically shook her hand to dislodge its hideous black blight.

And her screams pealed shrilly through the depths of the wood.

On his next free evening Timothy again went into town. He was acquiring a taste for wandering its streets at night. A taste for watching the young girls going by —particularly any who were unaccompanied.

This evening he had a number of things on his mind.

Yesterday's papers had reported the murder of a man found in the alley of The Rugged Staff public house. The report had mentioned that this was the second murder by strangulation which now awaited solution. It was over a year since the Stilford fortune-teller, Madam Riva, had been strangled in her residential caravan.

The mention of the previous strangling had caused Timothy a cynical smile. It would suit the police, of course, to imagine a link between the two stranglings. Then they would have only one strangler to look for instead of two. Still, they were welcome to think that—so long as it was the first strangler who got the blame for both killings!

Personally, Timothy doubted whether either of the killers would be in any danger from the Stilford C.I.D. Stilford police were out of their depth with any crime more serious than shoplifting. They'd failed to find the fortune-teller's killer even in a year. They would be equally unsuccessful in hunting the killer of that drunk in the alley.

After parking his car in a municipal car park, Timothy had a meal in a restaurant and then began his stroll.

A news-and-tobacco kiosk reminded him that he was out of cigarettes. He called in for a packet and for an evening paper.

He was about to leave with them, when he realised that he had been short-changed. A shilling short. He turned back to the counter, displaying the change he'd been given.

"Shilling short!" he said.

The scraggy proprietor shook his head.

"No, sir. Never make mistakes like that. Been in the trade too long."

"You calling me a liar?" Timothy asked.

"No, sir. Just mistaken, sir. Happen to anyone."

Timothy said nastily: "Anyone but you, eh?"

The tobacconist shrugged.

"It's the difference between the amateur an' the professional, sir. When you've been dealing with change every day of your working life——"

Timothy said: "I don't need a lifetime's experience in order to be able to subtract the price of a packet of cigarettes and a paper from a ten shilling note!"

The amount at issue was a small one, but the principle of the argument was becoming very important to him.

Obstinately the tobacconist said: "Maybe not, but this time you must have made a mistake. In any case, mistakes can't be rectified once the customer has left the counter!"

The man presented this clincher with a smug grin, as his trump card.

Timothy felt his blood-pressure rising. He felt a tension in his hands. His eyes studied the tobacconist's scrawny throat. That throat was fairly begging for the grip of his eager hands. How he'd like to meet this insolent tradesman in a dark alley!

For several seconds he fought to subdue the impulse that was seething through him. But to vent his feelings in this public place would be madness.

This situation, in fact, was the acid test of whether he really was mad. If he couldn't control and suppress a homicidal urge in a place like this, then he was no longer rational. No longer susceptible to any consideration but a lust to kill.

The tobacconist stood watching him, unaware of his nearness to violent death. And when the customer at last relaxed and turned to leave, the shopkeeper smirked.

Timothy said: "You've gained a dishonest shilling—and lost a customer!"

Patronisingly, the tobacconist suggested: "That shilling is probably in your pocket, sir. Now, if you'll excuse me——"

It was an insolent dismissal. But as Timothy went out his feeling was not one of humiliation. It was one of victory.

He didn't *have* to kill, then! He had had that fellow's life in his hands, but had spared him. He felt like a judge who had come to a merciful decision. The power of life and death was his—but this time, despite the provocation, he had allowed the offender to live.

It gave him a sense of magnanimity and virtue. Of mastery over his own impulses.

And then he unfolded the paper he had brought and looked at its front page. The main news item leapt into vivid prominence.

WOMAN FOUND DEAD IN WOOD

This afternoon Stilford Police released the news that last night the body of a young woman was found in Fratton Wood, eighteen miles from Stilford.

Death, it is understood, was due to foul play, but no further details will be issued until after the post-mortem examination.

The body was discovered by a teenage courting couple, who immediately notified the local police.

Carefully Timothy refolded the paper.

So Alison had been found! How long before her body would be identified?

This didn't change the basic situation, of course. It had been inevitable that she would be found sooner or later. And eventually identified. But how would her identity help the police to solve the mystery of who had killed her?

Even granted the sex motive, they had a whole male orchestra to consider as possible suspects. Not to mention casual strangers who could have followed and killed her.

So now the police had two recent murders on their plate. Alison's and the drunk's.

Just as well he was now in full control of his impulses. No more killings, whatever the provocation!

He walked back to the car park. And he arrived in time to see a young urchin deliberately scratching the glossy paintwork of his car!

With a bellow of fury, Tomothy ran at him.

The boy was alone. And as he ran towards him Timothy was aware that the car park seemed to be otherwise deserted.

With a rusty six-inch nail still in his hand, the boy swung round in alarm. In three more strides, Timothy had him by the throat.

"You destructive little brat!" he hissed. "I'll kill you!"

It was no idle threat.

There were only a few other cars in the park, and there were no other motorists to see as Timothy slammed the boy against the side of his car, his hands constricting mercilessly on the slender throat.

All his recent pride in his self-control was now forgotten. All that mattered to him—obsessed him—was the driving urge to avenge the damage done to his car.

The boy's eyes were already starting from his head.

His mouth was gaping. His knees were slackening, his small hands scratching feebly at the wrists of his killer.

Some semblance of caution made Timothy release one hand to wrench open a rear door of the car. Grabbing up the semi-conscious boy, he tossed him in on to the rear seat. Then he climbed in after him. With one knee on the bench seat to steady himself, he resumed his double grip on the boy's throat. And he did not release the grip till the boy was dead.

Then he dropped the body on to the floor, where it would be out of sight, climbed out of the car and got in again behind the steering-wheel.

He disposed of the body on his way back to Crestleigh. In a farm pond covered with green scum.

Only one person noticed his car parked beside the field. That person was his brother Matthew.

Matthew was driving back to Stilford after a visit to his father in quest of another cheque, when he recognised the number-plate of the stationary car.

Curious, he drove on a hundred yards, left his own car at the roadside and crept back to find out what Timothy was doing at night in such a deserted spot.

Concealed behind a roadside tree, Matthew saw Timothy climb over the fence from the field, re-enter his car and drive on towards Crestleigh. Matthew then climbed into the field, to search for whatever had interested Timothy.

There was nothing in the field but a cow pond in one corner, with a few trees near by. Matthew's attention was attracted by the disturbed scum on the surface of the pond. Had Timothy thrown something in there?

Among the trees Matthew found a long, dead branch and with it fished the area which was clear of scum.

The branch hooked in something—some sort of clothing. He tugged, and from where it had been held in the bottom mud he brought to the surface a fairly heavy weight. In the ghostly, diffuse light of the summer night, he saw a small human face break surface. The bloated, open-eyed face of a small boy, now streaked with green slime.

Matthew knew from previous experience the appearance of a person who had died of strangulation. That was how this boy had died.

And Timothy—the dedicated, righteous Timothy—must be his killer!

Using the branch again, Matthew pushed the body back under the surface. Knowing that it would soon float, because it had been dead when immersed.

Slowly he went back to his car. Carefully he drove back to his flat in Stilford.

And in his mind was one thought.

That midget Indian swami had promised him vengeance on those who had wronged him, the two people he hated. Timothy, possessor of his stolen hands, was now a killer. A killer who would be hunted by the Law.

Was that the form the swami's promised vengeance had taken? Was that the effect of his curse?

Matthew gave prolonged thought to the question.

But though he now knew Timothy to be a killer, he also knew that, as far as the Law was concerned, it was knowledge he had to keep to himself.

For he too was no stranger to murder!

"Come in!"

In response to the gruff invitation, Inspector Russell opened the door of the chief constable's office and walked in. The inspector was carrying a typewritten report.

"Result of the post-mortem, sir!" he announced, proffering the foolscap sheets. "Dr. Brent says that the girl's death was not due to the head injuries. They were inflicted after death."

"Then what *was* the cause of death?" Chief Constable Purvis inquired, from behind his neat desk.

"Asphyxia caused by manual strangulation," Russell said. He paused significantly. "That's three murders by strangulation now, sir. That fortune-teller a year ago, the fellow with a skinful of booze—and now this young woman. Though the young woman must have been murdered before the man was."

The Chief Constable held the report without reading it.

"You think, Russell, that one killer is responsible for all three murders?"

Russell frowned. "It's a natural temptation to think so, sir, because it would mean we'd only one killer to find, instead of three. The trouble is motive. There's no motive in common——"

The Chief Constable murmured: "The motive for the fortune-teller's murder appeared to be common robbery. That certainly didn't apply to the murder of the man found in the pub alley. He hadn't been robbed——"

"And it doesn't apply to this young woman found in the wood, sir. The post-mortem shows there was a sexual assault on her—and there are injuries which could only have been inflicted by a sadist." The inspector's tone was unusually grave. "Whether there's one killer or three, sir, the man who murdered that girl must be some kind of psychopathic monster. I don't mind admitting I shan't sleep easy as long as he's at large in Stilford."

The Chief Constable nodded in sympathy. "Same here. And we shall have the press howling about our crime record now. Quite justifiably." He laid down the post-mortem report. "Now, as you say, we mustn't jump to the conclusion that we've only one killer to find—even though it's quite possible. Pending further evidence, we must keep an open mind on that point. If there's just one strangler, why the year's interval after the first murder—and then two more stranglings in a week?"

"It's possible the killer's mania has just come to its pitch, sir——"

"Maybe. But the next thing, of course, is to try to get this murdered young woman identified."

Russell nodded. "Well, she's been dead for several days, sir, so we're naturally interested in any young women who've been missing during the last few days. In that connection I've an idea who the murdered girl may be."

"Oh?"

"That young woman Alison Garfield, sir! Secretary of the Philharmonic. The time factor and age would fit. I'm going to get the orchestra manager along to have a look at the body——"

Russell was interrupted by the shrilling of the telephone on the Chief Constable's desk.

The police chief picked up the handset and listened. As he did so, his ruddy face paled.

In a slightly uneven voice, he said into the phone: "All right. I'll send a squad car along straight away."

He cut off, dialled an internal number and issued the promised instruction. Then he replaced the handset and looked grimly up at Russell.

"Make that *four* stranglings, Inspector!" he said bleakly. "The body of a young boy has been taken out of a farm pond at Westbrooke Green. Death was due not to drowning—but to manual strangulation!"

For a long moment the two police officers gazed gauntly at each other. Then the Chief Constable slammed a fist down on his desk.

"So what motive in common is there now, Inspector? A female fortune-teller who was strangled and robbed but not sexually assaulted. A man who was strangled but not robbed. A young woman who was raped and strangled. Now a young boy—strangled and tossed into a pond."

"The only common factor being manual strangulation!" Russell was silent for a moment, rubbing thoughtfully at his square chin. Then he said: "But doesn't this latest strangling make it look as though there *is* one killer, sir? It's difficult to believe that there are four stranglers in Stilford. Looks to me more like one homicidal maniac running amok!"

"You mean, given the basic homicidal urge, he reacts homicidally to different kinds of provocation from different kinds of people—with strangulation as his favourite murder method!"

"Seems feasible, sir. And I think the public should be warned and asked to co-operate with us. It's difficult to believe that such a maniac can have committed four murders without in some way appearing abnormal to people he meets."

"I agree. Prepare a statement for the press, Russell. Then drop all other work and concentrate on this murder hunt. Ask me for any assistance or extra facilities you may need—but find this killer or killers before there are any more stranglings!"

That evening's *Stilford Echo* came out with a bold front-page bannerhead:

HUNT FOR STRANGLER

Beneath was a report of the murder wave now engaging the full investigating resources of the town's C.I.D.

> Stilford's good record as a town of law and order is now gravely blotted by four unsolved murders. These involve the deaths of two women, a man and a boy. And all four victims died from manual strangulation.
>
> One of these murders has features indicating serious mental abnormality in the killer, and the police believe that this abnormality may have revealed itself in other ways and be known to some member of the public.
>
> It is urgently necessary that the strangler or strang-

lers now at large be caught and put under restraint. Anyone with any knowledge or suspicion which might help the police in their inquiries is asked to get in touch with the Chief Constable at the Central Police Station, or to inform any police officer.

In an adjacent column was a detailed report of the finding of the murdered boy's body by the Westbrooke Green farmer. The young victim having been identified as eleven-year-old Terry Skuse, of the Spalding council estate.

In the three-star final edition of the *Echo* there was a Stop Press footnote to the day's police announcements.

STRANGLED GIRL IDENTIFIED

Early this afternoon the young woman found dead in Fratton Wood was identified as Alison Garfield, secretary of the Stilford Philharmonic Orchestra, who disappeared several days ago.

Mr. Denis Kendrick, manager of the orchestra, provisionally identified her by her clothing, and this identification has been confirmed by Miss Garfield's dentist. The murdered girl's dental condition corresponds with Miss Garfield's dental record.

Police inquiries are proceeding with all urgency, and C.I.D. leave has been cancelled.

10: Nightmare

"No, Alan!"

Timothy screamed.

He lay on his back, sweating. And as fast as the sweat beaded on his face and chest, it was dried up by the blasts of heat from the glaring furnace of the crematorium.

Heat haze blurred his vision, curling up to the unseen height of the vast furnace. And silhouetted against the lurid red glow stood a skeleton whose bones gleamed white through a tattered and smouldering black shroud.

He raised a skeletal hand to point it at Timothy—and a booming, accusing voice echoed and re-echoed hollowly through the incandescent vault.

But it was when the skull grinned malevolently at him that Timothy screamed. For although it was a fleshless skull, he knew that the face of the cadaver was that of his brother Alan.

That this was so, there came instant eerie proof. From among his charred tatters the skeleton produced a violin and bow. He lifted them and began to play.

Trills of gloating and menace. Sombre double-stopping chords that spoke of murder, damnation and the retribution of cosmic justice.

The fiddling skeleton danced nearer to the supine man, the glow behind him casting a long, accusing shadow.

Now, fiddling madly, he twirled around Timothy in a grotesque *danse macabre*. And his bony jaw moved to a hoarse, monotonous chant that was audible above the wail of the fiddle.

"*Murderer! Murderer! You killed my Alison. Strangler! You killed her . . . you killed her . . . !*"

The shadow of the skeletal fiddler now lay right across the sweating man.

"No, Alan!" Timothy shrieked. "No, Alan . . . !"

"*Liar!*" The skeleton hurled the word through fleshless jaws, and his bony fingers plucked nerve-twitching squeals from the fiddle.

Timothy struggled crazily . . . and got to his knees. The whole lurid tableau tilted . . . faded. He was on his feet.

And ahead of him, in leaden gloom, stretched the long, narrow road to a cemetery, with twin lines of cypress trees casting jet-black shadows across the path of the mourners.

On the still air hung the sound of sobbing . . . the heart-broken sobbing of bereaved parents. It came from the single coach following the hearse.

And the coffin in the hearse was small. Small enough to fit the corpse of a boy of about eleven.

Timothy tried not to follow the procession. He tried not to—but his legs and feet carried him close behind that slow-moving coach of mourners.

Suddenly, as the cemetery gate was looming up, one of the two people in the coach looked round through the rear window. It was a woman dressed in black, with tragic eyes peering out from a pallid, ravaged face.

She saw Timothy—and recognised him.

She raised an accusing hand to point at him through the glass.

And she cried in anguish: "*Killer! Murderer! You devil . . . you devil! Give me back my boy . . . !*"

Timothy shuddered. Her eyes were blazing like coals in the pallor of her hate-filled face.

"*You'll pay, you devil!*" she cried, and her words were vibrant with prophetic certitude.

Timothy could not break away. He kept pace with the procession as it passed through the lychgate.

And there, in the gloom, he saw the red earth of a row of newly-dug graves.

In one of them lay a large coffin. Even as the procession drew to a halt, Timothy saw the lid of the coffin rise. It tumbled aside—to reveal the occupant.

The open-eyed, bloated face of a man. A face bloated from drink—and from strangulation.

The open eyes found Timothy. The gross figure rose out of the grave. In horror, Timothy felt himself drawn towards it.

Then he saw that the bereaved parents had stepped out of the coach and were approaching him . . . converging on him. He found himself surrounded by them and the drunk he had murdered.

A bell began tolling. A mournful knell that hammered monotonously at his flinching brain. Now vengeful hands were clutching him . . . forcing him towards one of those newly-dug graves.

He protested shrilly. But, with remorseless strength, the three people dragged him to the centre grave. In it, he now saw, lay the figure of a young woman—surmounted by a bloody pulp which must once have been her head.

His scalp crawled. Her slender white arms were lifting to him in invitation. Her long fingers were beckoning.

From that bloody pulp bubbled words of crooning enticement.

"Come, my murderous lover . . . ! Come! You wanted my embrace . . . and here it is, awaiting you. Come, my lover. Kiss me . . . kiss me . . . !"

Gibbering with fear, Timothy was sent staggering down into the bed of clay and the receptive embrace of those dead but animate arms.

The gross drunk had lifted a spade and was preparing to shovel the clay earth down on the entwined couple.

But as Timothy sprawled, hands were at his throat. The hands of the bereaved parents.

Now the damp walls of the grave were enclosing him. Long cold white arms were encircling him. And another sound had now joined the tolling of the bell. The triumphant squealing of a fiddle.

Timothy felt himself choking. He felt himself being forced down, sucked down, into the earth's clay maw.

His ears were aching from the chaotic discords of bell and violin. His lungs were panting for air. His head throbbed . . . his heart pounded as if about to burst.

Through the tormenting cacophony sounded hate-filled accusations.

"*. . . Child-killer . . . ! My murderous lover . . . ! Strangler! Die . . . die . . . die . . . !*

He choked . . . sobbed with terror, sinking into a black, suffocating abysss. And through the murk a leprous hand reached out to grasp him. His guilty mind cowered.

"*You killed her!*" a voice thundered. "*My Alison—you murdered her. For that you'll burn in hell!*"

"No, Alan! No——!"

He shrieked again. And, still shrieking, he awoke abruptly in the darkness of his bedroom.

His pyjamas were clinging to his clammy body. His face was wet and cold with sweat.

Suddenly his bedroom door opened. Electric light dazzled him.

In the doorway stood his father.

"Timothy!" he said. "What's wrong? You've been shouting!"

Timothy lay panting. Frightened. It was a long time before he could speak.

"A—a dream!" he said huskily at last. "Just a dream. Must have been . . . overdoing things. . . ."

His father stared across the room at him.

"You're all right now?"

"Yes. All right now."

But when his father had switched off the light and gone, Timothy lay in the darkness cringing with terror.

Alone with his conscience, he relived his nightmare.

And fear was still with him when dawn showed palely through the window curtains.

"The Healing Sanctuary"

That was the lettering on the board beside the front door. Architecturally the building was a stone-built, bay-windowed house. It stood in the middle-class residential suburb of Elmside.

Timothy Lodway strolled hesitantly past the front gate, then came back. He had seen The Healing Sanctuary advertised in the local paper. He knew it was a place run by and for spiritualists. It claimed to provide spiritual healing of body and mind.

He was wondering if it could also supply healing of the guilty soul.

He knew enough psychology to realise that his nightmare of the preceding night had been caused by the guilt in his subconscious mind.

A man could repress conscious thoughts of guilt. Could repress all moral sense. But the very act of repression created an explosive potential in the depths of his subconscious.

Any force unnaturally bottled up was potentially explosive, and human emotions were no exception. Feelings of guilt which were not acknowledged and expressed must eventually burst out under their own pressure.

And that haunting dream had been an outburst of the guilt he had refused to acknowledge.

It had resulted in a fear which allowed the suppressed part of his mind—the part with a conscience—to assert itself again.

With each crime he had committed, this homicidal evil dominating his personality had strengthened its domination and more and more suppressed that part of his mind which had at first been appalled.

But now terror was reviving the suppressed side of his dual personality. A terror beyond the fear of legal punishment.

Now he was seeing his new nature in all its monstrous ugliness. Was seeing the hideous thing that his soul had become.

Could his conscience even now be salved? Could there be absolution even for the infamy staining his fear-filled soul?

If the answer was yes, surely that absolution must be found in some such place as this sanctuary of spiritual healing?

He had heard it said that no man was beyond redemption. If that was true, then surely it was in a place like this that the devil now dominating his soul and mind could be exorcised?

Possessed by a devil. To the ancient mystics that had been a familiar concept. Could possession by a devil explain the change that had so recently come over his own character and personality? If so, who better than these spiritualists to cast out the evil spirit corrupting him?

On the board beside the door he saw some smaller lettering. "Open Circle 7.30 p.m. daily."

He had only a vague idea of what an open spiritualist circle would be. He envisaged a number of people sitting in the dark around a table, with hands joined, drawing to themselves the spiritual healing power they claimed to be available to them.

If he could join such a circle and, without revealing his vile secrets, share the spiritual strength flowing into them . . . the strength which would enable him to resist this devil which was driving him deeper and deeper into damnation. . . .

It was now 7.20 p.m. Impelled by fear, by a need of help in wrestling with this demon possessing him, he pushed open the gate and walked slowly up the path to the open front door.

A yard past the doorstep was another door, half-glazed. It swung slowly open to his touch. He found himself in a silent hallway.

A little way along the hallway another door stood open. From it came the soft murmur of voices. The open circle would soon be in session.

He made his way to the open door. Just inside the room beyond, a man stood beside a rack of black-bound hymn books. At sight of the new arrival he smiled a greeting and proffered one of the books.

With a nod of thanks, Timothy accepted the book and stepped past the man into the room.

What he saw was quite unexpected. Considering that the room was in a private house, it was quite a large one. Its furnishing and fitments were like those of a nonconformist chapel.

There was a central aisle between two blocks of chairs arranged in rows. At the far end of the room was a raised platform. In its centre stood a plain table on which were two tall glass vases of cut flowers.

To the left of the platform was a harmonium. At this a bald-headed man was seated, studying the sheet music on the stand.

To the right of the platform was a pair of french windows, looking out on to a lawn surrounded by flower beds, colourful in the mellow evening sunshine.

The whole atmosphere was one of peace, of spiritual tranquillity.

Quietly he took a seat in a vacant back row. Now he looked at the other people present.

About half of the seats were occupied, and women outnumbered men by about two to one.

Automatically his eyes inspected them. His glance paused on a girl seated alone in a row otherwise entirely vacant. A teenage girl with a smooth complexion, and dark hair reaching to her shoulders.

There was a stir among the congregation. A side door had opened. A woman came through and mounted the platform, to stand behind the central table.

She was evidently the evening's presiding official. But there was nothing whatever in her appearance to suggest psychic gifts or even an interest in the occult.

Neither, Timothy realised, was there anything suggestive of the occult in the room itself. When the harmonium player played an introductory chord and then went into the opening bars of a hymn, the whole setting was again suggestive of a nonconformist chapel.

Timothy felt uneasy. Here were none of the things he had expected. No drawn curtains. No circle under cover of darkness or semi-darkness. The word "circle" had been quite misleading. Here was a public congregation, not a private sanctuary. Was it in this commonplace atmosphere that a man could find the occult power to fight a demon possessing him?

At the end of the introductory verse on the harmonium, the woman on the platform announced the hymn number. As the congregation sang, evening sunlight poured in through the french windows, intensifying the atmosphere of summer peace.

But the effect on Timothy was one of sour disappointment. He had not come here for this soothing syrup. He had come to wrestle in darkness with the powers of darkness; to draw on the deep well of the supernormal. This place was normal to the extent of being banal.

The woman on the platform could not have been more ordinary. In her late thirties, she was well-built and wore a smart, coral-pink dress. Her fair hair was stylishly set. About her throat was a double string of pearls and on her left wrist a gold watch.

As soon as the hymn came to an end, she began reading a series of announcements about regular members of the circle. Births, marriages, illnesses and deaths in their families.

Timothy could have laughed aloud in bitter irony. Here he sat among these people—a triple murderer, rent by internal conflict. Under the goad of fear, the better side of his nature had come to the surface—needing help to keep at bay the monstrous urges seeking to overwhelm it. And all he was getting was humdrum parish-magazine items of domestic news.

There was just one difference, however. When the woman announced a death, it was in no sombre manner. Instead, she said in a pleasantly conversational tone: "You will be interested to know that, after her long suffering, old Mrs. Brewster has now passed over. We wish her every happiness in the Summerland."

Again Timothy stirred uneasily. The psychic healing and strengthening power he needed were one thing—but this casual talk of immortality was another matter. The woman spoke so blithely and confidently about "passing over" to "the other side." But what awaited a triple murderer?

Having dealt with the mundane announcements, the woman now began to transmit messages from people who had actually passed over. Spirit messages to living relatives in the congregation.

Timothy had a strong urge to leave, but he was afraid to attract general and curious attention by doing so.

While transmitting the spirit messages, the woman still spoke in a pleasant, matter-of-fact tone. She didn't even close her eyes.

After several messages for older people, she announced one for someone named Claudine. The name was acknowledged by the solitary young girl Timothy had already noticed.

It transpired that she was a French *au pair* girl with a Stilford family.

The medium said: "The message is from Laurent. He asks me to quote a verse." In fluent French she enunciated a stanza of poetry. Before she had finished, the girl had broken down into soft sobbing.

With tears glistening on her cheeks, she at last looked up at the medium.

Huskily she muttered: "He . . . wrote that verse especially for me . . . !"

Timothy was badly frightened. This was almost worse than his nightmare.

The accusing mental spectres who had haunted his sleeping mind had been bad enough, but on waking he had recognised them as mere figments of his guilty subconscious. To sit here, however, and hear the dead spoken of as surviving entities—with their memories—sent a chill down his spine.

If the dead could remember a favourite poem, what could they *not* remember? And what message from the dead might this confounded medium quote next?

Then he forced a cynical smile. It wasn't from the dead that she'd been getting her "messages," of course. She was only quoting things known to members of her audience—like the verse recognised by the French girl.

She was simply practising telepathy. Telepathically she was picking up information from the minds of the living people in the circle, and mistaking its source.

Still—telepathy? His own mind, with its guilty secrets, was now present among her audience. If she could read that too . . . !

He began to get to his feet, intent on leaving. But he was arrested by a sudden change in the medium's tone and attitude.

No longer was she pleasantly conversational or sympathetic. In a hard, inflexible voice, she said:

"I have a strange feeling . . . ! With us tonight is someone alien to the peace of our circle. . . ."

Alarmed, Timothy began moving along the row, careless now of whether he was noticed or not, though he was relieved to see that the man in charge of the hymn books was no longer at the doorway.

All eyes in the congregation were fixed on the medium. In a loud, almost harsh, tone, she said:

"There is someone here who has no right to be here. I sense an evil influence. Someone among us is . . . *accursed!*"

The word hammered at Timothy's mind like the accusations in his nightmare. It transformed his own mood.

It was with a mental snarl that he passed out of the room. Quickly he went through the hallway and out of the front door.

He hurried down the path, left the gate swinging behind him, and turned along the pavement.

Then, in the shadow of a tree, he stopped. For several moments he stood with his head bowed, while conflicting fears and scruples and diabolical urges fought a battle in his mind. But the issue had really been decided even before he had come out of the house.

He crossed the road and took shelter in a shop doorway. From this he kept watch on the Healing Sanctuary.

Fear had now left him. So had all scruples and sense of guilt. If there were such a thing as retribution, he was damned beyond hope. But, on the principle that he might as well be hung for a sheep as a lamb, he could at least derive the utmost satisfaction from the urges with which he was cursed.

That woman had been right. He was accursed. Therefore he could not be held morally responsible for his actions. He grinned evilly. In a way, that *was* absolution! The repudiation in advance of personal responsibility for anything he might care to do.

As the evening darkened, he continued to watch, his mood cynical, self-indulgent, ruthless. His hands twined together in pleasurable anticipation.

That *au pair* girl. She had caught more than his eye. She had caught his interest—with an obsessive intensity.

Obviously she had arrived at the Sanctuary alone. So she should be leaving alone.

Again he gave an evil grin. Sanctuary! It was going to prove no sanctuary for her.

His temporary weakness, his squeamishness of conscience, were now overcome. But he was glad he had gone to the Sanctuary. That young *au pair* girl could make it more than worthwhile.

He waited for over an hour before the first member of the congregation appeared at the doorway.

And that first person to leave was the *au pair* girl!

This gave him a double satisfaction, because it meant that the medium hadn't kept her back to give her a private warning of danger. The blonde woman might be able to read the minds of the susceptible—but evidently she was no prophet!

He kept in cover till the *au pair* girl was walking along to the nearest bus-stop. Then he went after her.

As he overtook her, he was wondering just how long she would take to die.

11:
Blackmail for Two

MATTHEW LODWAY opened the outer door of his flat in response to a ring—and stared in surprise.

Smiling up at him from his diminutive height was the Indian midget who had called himself Swami Barham Lal Sivasan.

"Good evening, Mr. Lodway!" he greeted, in a tone that was almost a purr.

Matthew frowned angrily. He had hoped never to see the midget again. Had clung to this hope in spite of all instinctive forebodings.

But the little swami had discovered not only his name but his address.

Matthew demanded: "How did you know where to find me?"

Still smiling blandly, the Indian shrugged.

"Naturally, I mentioned you, by description, among the Nirvana Club members. That produced your name. And when I had been given your name it was easy for me to ask the club secretary for the address of my friend Mr. Lodway. I trust I am not unwelcome?"

"I . . ." Matthew hesitated, then decided to humour the man. "Of course not——"

The smile expanded. "In that case you will no doubt invite me in. Return my poor hospitality, so to speak!"

Matthew's frown deepened. So the midget had come to remind him about that evening. It was a disquieting nuisance. Still, they couldn't stand here at the doorway any longer.

"Yes—come in!" Matthew invited, stepping aside.

"Thank you!"

The midget trotted past him. Matthew followed him into the lounge, which the Indian inspected with interest.

Matthew said drily: "Not as exotic as your place, I'm afraid. And I don't happen to have any houris on the premises!"

The Indian grinned. "No matter! Then I must be content to accept your kind offer of a drink."

"Uh—yes. Scotch suit you?"

"Quite well, thank you!"

Matthew poured two whiskies and gave one to the swami.

"Afraid I can't offer you a reefer too!" he said sardonically.

"Then let me offer you one of mine." The Indian reached into the breast pocket of his neat suit for his cigarette case.

Matthew shook his head.

"No, thanks. I'd rather keep control of my faculties, if you don't mind."

The Indian left his cigarette case where it was and sat down on the settee. His feet didn't quite reach the carpet.

Still standing, Matthew frowned down at him.

"I suppose you've some particular reason for coming here? It isn't just a social call?"

"Only partly. Though I must admit to a little friendly concern on finding that you hadn't been to the Nirvana Club since the evening we met there. A suspicious man might have imagined you were trying to avoid him!"

Ironically Matthew said: "I appreciate your concern. But if this is only partly a social call——"

The swami gently swung his legs and sipped at his scotch.

"Principally," he said, "I've come about the two hundred pounds."

Matthew did a surprised double-take. "Two hundred pounds? What on earth——"

"Come!" the midget chided. "Don't tell me you've forgotten our little . . . business arrangement!"

Matthew put down his glass. His face was set and unamused.

"I don't recall any business arrangement," he said coldly.

For a fleeting second the Indian's good-humour faded. In his eyes glinted something very nasty.

"Let me refresh your memory," he said softly. "You admitted that evening that you would have like to have revenge on two people who had robbed you. I undertook to provide that revenge——"

Matthew cut in quickly: "But you said you wouldn't be doing it for payment!"

The Indian showed his teeth. "Then you do remember our conversation! That being so, you will remember me saying that my reason for helping you would not be primarily for financial reward. But I was careful to add that if future events should give you cause to be grateful to me, you could make a voluntary financial token of appreciation."

He emptied his glass and put it down beside Matthew's.

"Isn't that so, Mr. Lodway? And isn't it true that you agreed? You said that if I should fail to do what I was hinting at, you would owe me nothing——"

"Well—you *have* failed!"

The Indian was watching him closely.

"Have I? Anyway, I summarised our agreement. If nothing happened you would owe me nothing. If I succeeded you would pay me two hundred pounds."

Matthew scowled. "It was you who mentioned that sum. I didn't."

"One of us had to be specific, Mr. Lodway. And the sum was very reasonable. You must have thought so then, because you agreed to it. You even invited me to begin . . . proceedings in your presence——"

"And you refused. So how do I know you've done anything at all?"

The Indian sighed with just a suggestion of impatience. "You must judge by results, Mr. Lodway!"

"There aren't any."

The midget's smile again wore thin.

"That I find difficult to believe, Mr. Lodway." His eyes narrowed in a stare Matthew found strangely intimidating. "However, if nothing adverse has happened to your enemies, you will not object if the same kind of . . . ineffectual influence should be directed at *you?*"

Matthew was shaken. He licked his bottom lip and muttered uneasily: "Look here——"

Blandly the swami said: "You will remember my *assuras*—what might be called my household demons. If their attentions to the two people who robbed you have been quite futile, you will surely have no fear if you become the subject of similar . . . attentions?"

Matthew sat down, rather heavily.

"Look!" he said. "I don't believe in all this mumbo-jumbo. But if you think I really owe you something . . ." He hesitated. "I . . . don't mind giving you something for your trouble. But not two hundred pounds. That's impossible. I simply haven't got it!"

Swami Barham Lal Sivasan shrugged.

"Possibly not. But no doubt you will be able to raise it." He studied Matthew with a chilling calculation. "Let us say three days, eh? Then, if in three days you have not recompensed me for my . . . trouble, I shall have to consider myself wronged by you. In which case I shall have to confide my grievance to my *assuras*. . . ."

The threat was not one Matthew could take lightly. He was an eye-witness of the fact that in the last few days Timothy's life had been transformed. Transformed in a way that would have seemed incredible only a week ago.

Timothy, who had lost his hands because of his concern for a young boy in danger, had now become the murderer of another young boy. Could that radical change in his personality be entirely unconnected with the swami's curse?

If that curse could transform Timothy from a respectable and conscientious medical man to a hunted child killer, Matthew had no desire to discover what it could do to his own life—which already owed Justice an accounting for two murders.

"I—I'll do my best to raise the money," he muttered. "But it isn't going to be easy——"

"Easy or difficult, do make sure that you do not forfeit my . . . friendship. You need not bring the money to my restaurant. As a safeguard against the chance of your forgetting to deliver it to me, I shall call here three evenings from now . . . to collect your voluntary contribution!"

For a moment the bland smile again faded and Matthew was allowed a glimpse of the personality behind the genial mask.

Killer as he himself was, he felt a twinge of fear.

The midget slid off the settee on to his feet.

"Till then," he said quietly. "Thank you for the drink. Good-night!"

Matthew escorted him out of the flat. With the outer door relocked, he returned to the lounge and poured himself another drink.

Two hundred pounds! How could he raise that amount in three days? His financial creed had been: "Easy come, easy go."

His car wasn't paid for. It was only two days since he'd

had a cheque from his father—and that had been owed before being received. Which left only Timothy to "touch."

But—two hundred! After what Timothy had been doling out to him during the past year he wouldn t have that much money to spare.

Not willingly!

Matthew's face turned ugly. Willingly or not, Timothy would have to produce two hundred pounds.

Matthew's scowl changed to a sardonic grin. The idea began to appeal to him. There would be a certain mordant humour in making Timothy pay for the curse of which he was himself a victim!

And Timothy would have no choice in the matter. Not Timothy the child-killer. Not Timothy who had tossed a strangled boy into a pond and then driven home quite unconcerned. Timothy, who hid the secret of his guilt while the press clamoured for justice.

Matthew nodded decisively. Blackmail was the technical term for what he proposed to do—but blackmail was no worse than child-murder. And, with only three days in which to raise the money, there was little time to waste.

No time at all, in fact. A sudden thought gave the matter urgency.

The killer of that boy was being hunted—and Timothy might not be as lucky as his killer-brother had been. If the police were going to get on Timothy's track, he, Matthew, wanted to get to him first.

Quickly he finished his drink. He hurried out of the flat and fetched his car from the garage.

In a mood of implacable determination he drove out to Crestleigh.

Trapping Claudine, the *au pair* girl, proved very easy indeed.

She was the only person waiting at the bus-stop when Timothy approached her.

With his cool professional manner, he said: "Excuse me, but if you're going my way perhaps I can offer you a lift? I saw you in the Healing Sanctuary——"

She turned to look at him. Illogically, but as he had calculated, his reference to the Healing Sanctuary seemed to justify his self-introduction now.

"Oh—you were there!" she said, smiling.

The fact appeared to be accepted as an automatic guarantee of his trustworthiness, to prevent any suspicion even crossing her mind—despite the recent news stories of murders in Stilford.

This did not surprise him. Only one of the victims had been a young woman—and, anyway, murder was one of the things which happened to other people, never to oneself. As a doctor he knew that even serious illness ususually came as a surprise to the victim, as one of the misfortunes associated with other people or read of in medical books, not to be expected as a personal experience.

Murder was even more specifically one of those calamities one read about in the press, but with which one never came into personal contact. Murderers were shadowy, unreal, melodramatic figures. It never occurred to one that this real, living, pleasant-mannered person one was actually talking to could be a killer.

Every week young women accepted lifts from complete strangers—and were unutterably surprised when the sequel added to the list of rape reports in the Sunday papers. The fact that for years previously they had read numerous accounts of similar things happening to other young females made no difference to their readiness to trust a stranger.

After a drink and a chat with him in a pub, a man was no stranger. How much less was he a stranger when he had met one in a place like the Healing Sanctuary, with its circle of earnest, spiritually-inclined people.

Timothy returned her smile and said: "Yes, I was

there. I hated to see you so upset by your message. It was your first time there?" Considering the nature of the message and her emotional reaction to it, that was a safe guess. Had she been there before she would have received that message before and "communication" would not have been such an upsetting novelty.

"My first time," she admitted. "You are a regular member?"

"Quite an old stager!" he told her. The fact that she hadn't been to the Sanctuary before made that lie, too, a safe one.

She said: "I'm waiting for a bus to Cornwallis Road, Bruton——"

Fate was playing into Timothy's eager hands. Bruton was on the far outskirts of Stilford—virtually in the country. And buses to Bruton, being part of the "country" service, ran only once an hour.

He glanced at his watch. "I'm afraid you'll have a long wait for a bus. Next one isn't due for another forty minutes." He indicated the time-table on the bus-stop post.

She gave a rueful nod. "I know. A nuisance!"

He grinned reassuringly. "Fortunately it doesn't matter. I'm going that way——"

She glanced round for his car.

"Just across the road," he said, interpreting her glance.

She gave him a relieved and grateful smile. "It's very kind of you."

"Come along, then."

He took her elbow and led her across the road.

"Better introduce myself properly," he said chattily. "My name's Lodway. Dr. Timothy Lodway."

Supplying his real name involved no danger. She wasn't going to live to make use of it. And he calculated that the title "Doctor," again illogically, would inspire extra confidence.

He was right. She didn't know that Jack the Ripper was believed to have been a doctor. She knew nothing of the Landrus and Ruxtons and many other killers with medical degrees.

"Doctor!" she said, and became visibly friendlier.

He realised that the good looks he shared with Matthew were also lubricating the acquaintanceship.

He helped her into his car and climbed in beside her—inwardly smiling cynically at the fable of feminine intuition.

How many women would have gone trustingly to their violent deaths if intuition had been a general feminine gift?

On the drive through the dusk of Stilford he was filled with an inner excitement which he kept under control.

Now the die was cast, he was conscious of a strange sense of contentment. No more harrowing conflicts of conscience. No more fears, no more scruples. The world was a jungle and it was his destiny to be one of its predators.

The human race, like the animal species, consisted of two kinds. The hunters and the hunted. It was his good fortune to be a predatory male, and it was this trusting French girl's misfortune to be an attractive female.

Still, it would soon be over for her and she would join the countless millions of creatures who had died because of the inexorable jungle laws of life. Nature made no provision for sentimentality.

The location of Cornwallis Road made suspicious subterfuges unnecessary.

Before the exclusive residential area of Bruton was reached there was a stretch of undeveloped rural suburbia, which was quite convenient to his purpose. There was no need to drive past Bruton into the country proper nor to turn off the correct route. What had to happen could happen here—while he was still on the correct route but without continuing to Bruton.

The street lights of Stilford town were now far behind.

This twilit road was as deserted as the region in which Alison Garfield had died.

By a quick stab at the brake pedal without declutching, he managed to stall the engine, then allowed the car to coast to a stop, its evident lack of power preventing any immediate suspicion.

Shaking his head ruefully, he turned disarmingly to the *au pair* girl.

"Well—what d'you think of that!" he smiled.

And his hands reached for her throat.

She was no match for the practised hands that had already killed three people. He choked her into unconsciousness, then carried her into a roadside meadow.

She regained consciousness in a dark spinney on the far side of the field. Her attempted screams were smothered.

When he had finished with her, he rolled her body into the ditch beside the perimeter hedge, and tossed the remnant of her clothing in after her.

He was humming softly while taking a circuitous road home to Crestleigh, by-passing the town.

But it was not by intent that this route spared him the necessity of passing the farm on which he had dumped the murdered body of a boy two evenings ago. That incident had passed from his mind, superseded by tonight's more gratifying killing.

He made good time to Crestleigh. Expertly he negotiated the drive to the house.

His brows slanted when he recognised the dark bulk of Matthew's car parked beside it. Now that Alison Garfield was known to be dead and incapable of talking, Matthew had resumed his visits here!

Timothy almost laughed. Poor, bungling Matthew. How easily Alison had escaped him. How much more proficient she had found a professional man!

But Timothy was getting tired of doling out cheques to Matthew. He no longer felt guilty about having Matthew's hands. He no longer felt guilty about anything at all.

Matthew was too stupid and unenterprising to deserve hands anyway, and he couldn't go on making financial capital out of his loss. His sponging had to stop.

Timothy went indoors. As expected, he found Matthew in the lounge, seated at ease with a drink. Evidently he still had his key to the house.

"Hullo!" Timothy said sourly, from the doorway. "Whose turn is it this time—mine?"

"Turn?" Matthew said, affecting incomprehension.

"Whose turn to have his ear pulled!" Timothy amplified crudely.

Matthew's eyes glinted. This was a new attitude in Timothy. Another of the changes in him. But Matthew suppressed his resentment.

"Matter of fact, I *could* do with a sub!" he admitted.

"You don't say!" Timothy grinned sarcastically. "And how much would satisfy you this time?"

He strolled across the room to the cocktail cabinet.

Matthew kept his composure.

"Oh—two hundred would do!"

Timothy wheeled quickly round from the cocktail cabinet to stare at him.

"Two hundred pounds! Are you mad?"

Holding his glass between his two artificial hands, Matthew said suggestively: "That's a question I could ask you. Perhaps we're both mad. But I'm not a child-killer!"

Timothy stood motionless, as though suddenly paralysed. His hands, slightly hooked, hung at his sides. His eyes, looking down at his brother, were suddenly remote, impersonal.

After a long moment of silence he exhaled a rasping breath.

And then he stepped slowly towards Matthew.

12:
Vision of Evil

A YARD AWAY from Matthew, Timothy came to a stop.

"And what," he asked in a whisper, "does that mean?"

With his black-gloved artificial hands resting lightly on the chair-arms, Matthew leaned forward, ready to spring up. His gaze held that cold gaze of Timothy's.

"It means," he said deliberately, "that I know who killed that boy found in the pond at Westbrooke Green!"

There was a tense hiatus while Timothy absorbed the implications of the statement.

Then he challenged: "That person being——?"

"You! Dr. Timothy Lodway—favourite son of Stilford's gifted surgeon Virgil Lodway!"

Timothy gave a tight, gaunt grin.

"You really are mad!"

Calmly, Matthew said: "Two nights ago I saw you dump the body in that pond!"

Again a sibilant emission of breath from between Timothy's teeth.

"So . . . ! And, just supposing that it wasn't merely an hallucination of yours or invention of yours—why have you said nothing about it till now?"

Matthew said unctuously: "Blood is thicker than water!"

Timothy's grin was sarcastic. "Blood is thicker than water—till you think of a way of getting two hundred pounds, eh? A news item in the paper suggests to you that by inventing a fantasy about it and exerting a little unbrotherly pressure, you might make a profit!"

Relaxing, Matthew shrugged. "That's putting it the wrong way round. I had my knowledge about that murder before I needed two hundred pounds. It was my need of the money that brought me here. That need is as vital as yours. You need my silence. I need two hundred pounds. We can't afford to quarrel!"

"Can't we?" Timothy looked surprised. "If there were any truth in what you've been saying—that I killed that boy—don't you think you'd be a little rash to try to blackmail me?"

Still keeping an eye on his seated brother, he returned to the cocktail cabinet and poured himself a whisky and water.

Matthew asked coolly: "Are you trying to scare me?"

"No—just pointing out an obvious fact of logic!" Setting down his glass, Timothy lifted his hands for Matthew to see. "If you're right, and these hands killed that boy—why should a blackmailer be safe?"

Matthew's mouth twisted contemptuously: "Because the blackmailer *isn't* a boy!"

Timothy ignored the jibe. His brows drew together.

"After all," he said, "from what I've heard about blackmailers, they're never satisfied with just one payment. Once the victim submits, he's bled repeatedly." He paused. "As last he's probably driven to resist or hit back——"

"Is he?"

"But that's a foolish time to decide to resist—after he's been bled white and driven to desperation. It would be much more sensible to resist without paying anything! To resist in a mood of unemotional commonsense."

Matthew twisted in his chair and gave a faint grin.

"But can a killer afford unemotional commonsense? There must be something quite emotional in the prospect of being arrested for murder!"

Timothy sipped his drink and raised his eyebrows in feigned surprise.

"You'd have your own brother arrested for murder—and cause your father the disgrace and sorrow?"

Matthew said cynically: "I thought you were dealing in unemotional commonsense, not sentimental twaddle!"

He lifted his artificial hands.

"Aren't you forgetting that it was my affectionate father who robbed me of my hands—for the benefit of my child-killing brother? I hate your guts and his." Watching Timothy closely, he added: "It would serve him right to know what a use you've made of the hands he stole and gave you!"

Timothy leaned against the cabinet and laughed. "There's only your unsupported word that I had anything to do with that boy. That I've ever set eyes on him. Why should I have harmed him? What motive could I have?"

Matthew said: "Some killers don't need much of a motive. And I've been thinking since I saw you get rid of that boy's body. . . ."

There was a sudden tension in his attitude. It communicated itself to Timothy, who stood suddenly rigid, expectant.

"You've been thinking?" he invited, his face strongly controlled.

"Yes." Matthew's eyes narrowed, intent on his brother's face. "That boy died of strangulation. And he's not the only person in Stilford who's been strangled recently. One of the others was known to us. Known to you! Alison Garfield. . . ."

Timothy again moved to within a few feet of Matthew.

"And what does that signify?" he retorted. "She was known to hundreds of people—including you!"

"True. But she was perfectly all right last time I saw her——"

Impetuously Timothy jibed: "Only because she was quick enough to get away from you!"

Matthew's narrowed eyes opened a little wider. His mouth curved in a grim grin.

"So—you did see her after I did!" He half-rose from his chair. "You must have seen her, to know that!"

"Nonsense. After she got away from you, she phoned me that evening to tell me she wouldn't be coming here again—because of your attack on her!"

"Which proves she was all right when she left me! Whether she told you by phone or in person, it proves she was all right when she left me!" Matthew's voice began to mimic Timothy's words of a few moments ago. "And we've only your unsupported word that it was by phone that she told you! She may have seen you to tell you—and you may be the last person to have seen her alive!"

Timothy scoffed. "May—may! And you may have gone after her again after she spoke to me—to finish what you'd begun in this room. It's a known fact that you attacked her here——"

"No!" Matthew mimicked again. "There's only your unsupported word for that too! What a cheap bluffer you are. I know Alison was all right the last time I saw her, so I know the police can't prove otherwise. You stupid fool. I saw you dump that boy's murdered body—I'm an eye-witness! This is no bluff. It only needs an anonymous tip-off to the police. They won't neglect any hint in a murder case!"

Matthew came up out of his chair, to face Timothy

on his feet. Matthew's words were rapid with conviction.

"They say every criminal has his own method, his *modus operandi.* It becomes his trade-mark. It's a bit of a coincidence, isn't it, that that boy's killer and Alison Garfield's killer had the same trade-mark—murder by strangulation! How would you like the police to begin investigating your activities during the Stilford stranglings?"

Timothy turned paler. It was a reaction he could not prevent.

His voice glutted with venom, he snarled: "You meddling fool. If I really killed that boy and Alison, d'you think I'd have any compunction about shutting your mouth?"

Matthew stood his ground. He said contemptuously: "I'm not as easy to kill as a woman or a boy—or a drunk!"

He added the final words on an automatic impulse, because the press had been blazoning the three stranglings. But the effect of those words on Timothy—a startled and frightened flinching—caused Matthew to step towards him triumphantly.

"My God!" he whispered. "It's true, then. You murdered that poor devil too!" He gave a victorious grin. "Well—that makes two hundred pounds a very cheap price for shutting my mouth!"

Timothy moved closer to him. His eyes glinted with a bitter humour that was not quite sane.

His voice husky with pent-up hate and rage, he said viciously: "Eight fingers and two thumbs are a lot cheaper!"

And he hurled himself at Matthew and got his hands about his throat. With maniacal strength he slammed Matthew down across the chair he had recently occupied.

Getting a knee to Matthew's midriff, he exerted all the power of his forearms to drive those fingers and thumbs deeper into his brother's throat.

He gave a gurgling laugh. "Funny, isn't it, Matthew? A blackmailer being strangled with his own hands! Feel them choking the life out of you . . . ?"

Matthew was floundering helplessly, his eyes bulging, his artificial hands flailing the air.

Timothy went on babbling. "Feel them? They were once part of your own body, Matthew—and now they're going to make a corpse of it! Now they're going to shut your blabbing mouth for ever . . . !"

His face contorted with murderous glee, he drove his knee deeper under Matthew's rib-cage and as the pinned body slackened he got the imprisoned throat across a chair-arm.

Now he knew he had his victim helpless for the kill. Clenching his teeth and slitting his eyes with the effort, he rammed power into the strangling, grafted hands.

In Chief Constable Purvis's office, Inspector Russell swung round from his chief's desk as a tap sounded on the door. The door opened and a uniformed constable put his head into the room.

"A lady wants to see you sir. Says it's urgent."

Irritated by the interruption, the Chief Constable shot a quick glance at the intruder. "It had better be! Who is she?"

The constable said: "She's a Mrs. Claremont—of The Healing Sanctuary."

"And what has she come about?"

The constable hesitated before answering.

Then he said: "She believes she may have seen a murderer this evening!"

Chief Constable Purvis made a very prompt decision. "Bring the lady in, Vowles," he ordered crisply.

The constable disappeared and a minute later reappeared escorting a smartly dressed, blonde woman in her late thirties.

When the constable had again vanished and the woman

had seated herself in the chair pulled forward by Inspector Russell, Purvis said:

"My constable told me something rather surprising, Mrs. Claremont. I suppose he got it right? That you think you've seen a murderer this evening!"

Composedly Mrs. Claremont said: "It isn't a question of thinking. The use of the conscious mind hampers the faculty of psychic insight——"

"Er—quite! But you . . . feel that someone you've seen this evening may be a murderer!"

Equably the blonde woman said: "I would put it more strongly than that. I *know* a man I saw this evening is a murderer. But from your viewpoint, I realise, there'll be a 'maybe' in the matter."

Chief Constable Purvis looked at her steadily. "Suppose you give me the details of what happened?"

"Certainly. In the Sanctuary this evening I was relaying spirit messages to people in the open circle from relatives and friends who had passed on."

She said this as matter-of-factly as though she were a post office telegraphist referring to a message transmitted by wire.

"And——?"

"I'd just given a message to a young French girl from her sweetheart on the other side—when I received vibrations of a most appallingly evil kind!"

Inspector Russell coughed to cover his discomfort at this unfamiliar terminology of the immaterial. But in the absence of concrete evidence concerning the murders engaging the police investigators, even the most unsubstantial hint had to be given attention. So the Chief Constable gave the medium an encouraging nod.

Calmly she continued. "I had the sense of someone among the people present being . . . accursed . . . !"

"Accursed!" Russell blurted.

"Yes. Or, if you prefer, of being under a most malevolent influence. And I was impelled to announce the fact. I expressed the feeling that someone present had no right to be there . . . someone alien to the peace of our circle . . ."

"Please go on."

"Well, just before I got that feeling, a man in the back row was getting up to leave. A man I had never seen before——"

"Let me get this straight!" the Chief Constable broke in. "He was leaving before you made this announcement—so it couldn't have been that which made him leave!"

"I suppose not. He was almost at the door when I spoke of someone accursed. And when he had gone I was conscious of a great sense of relief—as of the departure of something evil——"

"Ah, yes . . . !" the Chief Constable commented vaguely. "But why did you conclude that he was a murderer—if he *is* the person you referred to as such?"

"He is the person. But I was not aware of it at the time. You see, the impact of those vibrations, coming on top of my contact with the serenity of the Summerland——"

"Summerland?" Russell inquired.

"The other side!" Mrs. Claremont explained patiently. "As I was saying . . . the clash of those malign vibrations with the tranquillity of the Summerland left me in what might be called a psychic turmoil——"

"You were getting your lines crossed!" Russell suggested.

Mrs. Claremont frowned.

"Put crudely—yes. I felt weak and ill. So I had to wait till the meeting was over to retire to a private room for a deep trance——"

"Oh . . . !" Russell muttered, sparing the Chief Constable a wry glance.

His chief was nothing if not diplomatic.

He said urbanely: "And it was in this deep trance after the meeting that you realised the strange man had been a murderer?"

Mrs. Claremont flashed him a smile in appreciation of his understanding.

"Exactly. But, more than that . . . I saw the method of his abominable crimes——"

"And that's——?" Purvis prompted.

"I saw a pair of hands . . . masculine hands. They gave me a sense of overpowering evil. And when I saw them at close range I knew why. The thumbs told me that they were the hands of a murderer or potential murderer——"

"Thumbs!" The two police officers exchanged startled glances.

"Yes. People's personalities and characters, you know, are written in their hands——"

Russell cut in: "But that's palmistry. I didn't know it had anything to do with your line—I mean with spiritualism."

"Actually it hasn't. There's nothing psychic in palmistry. It's a science anyone can learn. But I am interested in all means of enlightenment regarding the human personality. I know that the clubbed thumbs I saw on the hands in my trance are a sign of a brutal nature and an ungovernable temper—of blind, uncontrolled passion aroused by the slightest opposition. Such thumbs have been found on the hands of many murderers guilty of crimes of passion. But that wasn't all——"

"Oh?"

"No. On the mount of Saturn, just below the second finger, I saw a star——"

"And what does that signify?"

"According to the late Cheiro, the greatest of all palmists, it indicates a distinction to be dreaded. A person with such a star usually leads an abnormal life and comes to a violent end. In conjunction with the clubbed thumbs, the homicidal significance is unmistakable. And my trance gave confirmation of this."

"In what way?"

"I saw those hands take hold of a bare human throat and choke it. And later I saw a man's distant shadowy figure, carrying what was obviously a body into the depths of a wood——"

The two men frowned. This last vision was no more than could have been gleaned from the newspaper reports of the Alison Garfield murder.

"And that's all?" Purvis asked.

"No. When that shadowy figure reappeared from the wood it was as if he were coming towards me. I could see his face—and it was the face of the man who had hurried out of my meeting. And in the trance vision he lifted his hands to look at them—and I saw that they had the club-tipped thumbs I had already seen."

The two police officers were silent. At last Purvis inquired: "Nothing else?"

"Except for my feeling that the man's evil hadn't ended. That there was more violence and death to come."

"Mmm." The Chief Constable was looking down at his desk, musing. Then he looked up at the blonde woman. "Mrs. Claremont—I'm going to be quite frank."

"Please do."

"Well—all this is unsubstantial in the extreme, isn't it? Where we are concerned, palmistry itself is unsubstantial enough—and those sinister hands you saw weren't even real, flesh-and-blood hands. They were only a vision in a trance. But you're implying that the man who left your meeting had such hands!"

"I feel sure of it!"

"But you didn't see his actual hands?"

"No."

"What about his actual face. What sort of man was he?"

"In his late twenties, I'd say. Good-looking, with blond hair."

"You know nothing else about him—his name, where he lives, etcetera?"

"I'm afraid not. He was a complete stranger. But after the trance I knew I had to come to you. You're looking for a terrible man who has been strangling people."

"But you can supply no personal details about this man of yours—even from your er—trance vision!"

"No. He seemed to be cloaked in evil, so that it was difficult to penetrate the blackness." Mrs. Claremont hesitated. "There was just one thing . . . which I don't understand. . . ."

"Yes?"

"In the trance I had a glimpse of what looked like surgical instruments. I don't say this man uses such instruments personally—though he may do—but I did get the impression that they somehow concern him."

"I see . . ." The Chief Constable gave no indication of what was passing through his mind. Instead he gave a smile and said: "Well—if that's all you can tell us, Mrs. Claremont——"

She took the hint and began to get up. "I'm afraid it is. Not much help to you?"

"Who knows? Even a suggestion may have value. Thank you, anyway, for taking the trouble to come here. What you have said will be given due attention." Purvis glanced at the inspector. "See Mrs. Claremont out, will you?"

Russell escorted her out. It was several minutes before he returned alone—and when he did his face was flushed with excitement.

"Let 'em all come!" he blurted, as he flung the door wide.

"What?" The Chief Constable stared.

"Another woman to see you, sir—and she goes one better!" The inspector paused, eying his chief for an expected reaction to what was to come. "Wait for it, sir . . . !"

"Spit it out, man!" Purvis barked impatiently.

Russell got it out, sardonically certain that he was going to surprise.

"This woman, sir, claims that she'd had the strangler's hands at her own throat!"

13:
Throat Man

The Chief Constable looked across his desk at the woman who had taken the place of his recent visitor. This woman had dark hair, an attractive face and a shapely figure, and he estimated her age to be about thirty.

"Now let me understand this clearly, Mrs. Matheson," he said. "You're not making a specific charge against your doctor. But you do think there's something strange about him——"

Mrs. Matheson cut in with a hint of reproach.

"It's at your own request that I'm here! In the paper last evening it said that this murderer you're looking for must have revealed some abnormality in other ways. And it asked anyone with any knowledge or suspicions that could help the police to get in touch with the Chief Constable."

"That's so."

"Well—as I've told you, there's something abnormal about my doctor. I'm telling you this in confidence, mind—so if I get sued for slander you won't find other people coming forward to help you."

"There's no question of that, Mrs. Matheson," Inspector Russell assured her. "You're doing a public service by volunteering information and—unless you charge someone with a definite criminal offence—anything you say is strictly confidential."

Mrs. Matheson relaxed. "That's all right, then."

"And this abnormality you've noticed in your doctor?" the Chief Constable asked. "Just what is it?"

She hesitated. "Well—you could say I didn't like what he did to my throat the other morning!"

Purvis leaned forward with interest. He repeated the request he had recently made to Mrs. Claremont. "Please give me details!"

"Very well." She arranged herself more comfortably in her chair. "I'd told him about my headaches—I suffer agonies with them, you know——"

"Yes. Please go on."

"Well, I told him how the muscles at the back of my neck seemed all knotted up. So he went behind me to feel the back of my neck. He put his hands here——" She raised one of her own hands to the nape of her neck.

"First he examined my neck with his fingers and thumbs, to see if there was anything wrong. That was normal enough. But then suddenly——" She paused, her eyes angry at the recollection. "Suddenly he rammed his thumbs hard into the back of my neck and gripped the sides of my throat as if . . . as if he was going to strangle me!"

An exchange of glances between the two police officers.

Tactfully the Chief Constable said: "Please don't misunderstand me, Mrs. Matheson, but one must be certain about such a serious matter. Are you quite sure that the newspaper reports of the stranglings and our appeal for information haven't caused you to . . . exaggerate a perfectly normal medical examination into something sinister?"

Mrs. Matheson frowned indignantly.

"Exaggerate? Certainly not. If you'd been examined by as many doctors as I have, you'd know whether an examination was normal or not. I've been thinking about it, haven't I, ever since I read your appeal, as you call it, in the paper. I didn't rush here as soon as I'd read it!"

"I appreciate that——"

"Then you can believe this. What he did to my throat was no normal examination. It *was* sinister! It made me cry out with the pain. And even then he didn't let go. I had to wrench myself away!"

The two police officers were now looking very serious. If this woman was not romancing, what had happened had at least been sufficiently unusual to be worthy of attention.

Mrs. Matheson went on: "I told him he'd hurt me. And he just stood there, with his fingers still crooked from how he'd gripped me—and there was a look in his face as if the devil was in him!"

The two men frowned. That final melodramatic phrase would have tended to weaken the conviction of what she'd been saying, have suggested a natural inclination to dramatise situations—had they not only recently heard another woman speak of a malevolent influence surrounding a suspected man. Now the one sinister description seemed to be an echo of the other.

"Did he offer any explanation?" Inspector Russell inquired.

"I demanded one! And he said he'd just been trying to relieve the muscular cramp. He said cramp in the leg could be relieved by pricking the muscle with a needle, and that he'd been trying a similar method to release the muscular tension in my neck."

"And you accepted that explanation?" The Chief Constable eyed her intently.

"I had to accept it, hadn't I—at the time! What else could I do? But privately I didn't swallow it even then.

And when I read what the paper said about this strangler probably showing abnormalities——"

"You did quite right to come here. Now . . ." Purvis spoke very seriously. "You specifically asked your doctor to examine your neck, and he could hardly do that without touching it——"

Mrs. Matheson got to her feet. "There are different ways of touching a person's neck—and I didn't like his way. I'm getting myself another doctor——"

"Please let me finish, Mrs. Matheson. Tell me—with a due regard for the gravity of what you say. Do you seriously think that your doctor actually would have strangled you—there in his surgery—if you hadn't wrenched away?"

Tartly she said: "Maybe not. He might have come to his senses in time anyway. But I didn't come here to tell you what I think. Only what happened. The thinking's up to you. But, since you've asked my opinion, I do think that doctor finds it difficult to keep his hands off some people's throats!"

She turned and moved quickly to the door.

Rising, the Chief Constable called urgently after her. "Just a moment, Mrs. Matheson! Please give us the doctor's name and description."

Pausing only briefly in her stride, she looked back over one shoulder and said laconically:

"He's just under thirty, good-looking and has fair hair. His name is Lodway. Dr. Timothy Lodway!"

Inspector Russell hurried after her to escort her to the exit and soothe her ruffled feelings on the way. When he returned to the office he found his chief running his fingers through his grey hair and showing signs of suppressed excitement.

"Well, sir," Russell inquired, "what d'you make of all that?"

The Chief Constable began jerkily pacing the room.

"I never thought, Russell, that we'd ever be reduced to working on the intuitions of a trance medium and the hunches of a hypochondriac. But I'm much more impressed than I wanted Mrs. Matheson to realise. There are several points we can't ignore—because they can't all be sheer coincidence."

"You mean—that medium tonight quoting palmistry . . . while the first strangled victim we know of was a palmist. Is it possible, sir, that it was because she was a palmist that Madam Riva was murdered? That she'd guessed too much about the man who killed her?"

"Well, I can imagine that the medium who came here tonight would have been in danger if what she suspects is true and the man concerned realised just how much she did suspect from a vision of his hands! But we've a series of striking coincidences——"

"Mrs. Claremont gets a vision of surgical instruments—and, quite independently, Mrs. Matheson suspects her doctor."

The Chief Constable nodded. "Next, the man who left the Healing Sanctuary in such a hurry was good-looking, blond-haired and in his late twenties—while Mrs. Matheson's suspect doctor is good-looking, fair-haired and just under thirty!"

Inspector Russell's eyes were glittering. In a voice oddly pitched, he said: "It's the other coincidence that shook me, sir. I've already questioned Dr. Timothy Lodway about one of the murder victims—when she first disappeared! Alison Garfield, the young woman found strangled in Fratton Wood, had been the fiancée of Dr. Lodway's late brother. Up to the time she disappeared she'd still been a frequent visitor to the Lodway house!"

The Inspector moved across to his chief's desk to pick up the internal telephone. "What's the odds, sir, against all those coincidences in combination by sheer meaningless chance?"

The Chief Constable said grimly: "That's right, Russell, ring for a car. The odds are great enough for us to pay a visit ourselves to Dr. Lodway's home! Where is it?"

"Out at Crestleigh, sir," Russell answered while he dialled. Then he swung to face his chief again.

"Which gives us one more coincidence, sir!" he said in a taut whisper. "On the way there we shall pass the farm where young Terry Skuse's body was found!"

Lying pinned across the chair-arm, Matthew Lodway glared up into the contorted face close above him.

Floundering like a landed, suffocating fish, Matthew fought to breathe—suffering the agonies he himself had inflicted on two people.

The imminence of death set his mind working desperately for a way to throw off this homicidal burden. To dislodge the murderous hands that had his throat in a relentlessly tightening grip.

His artificial hands went up and grasped the wrists of the man trying to kill him. He exerted his own failing strength—but the artificial hands were impotent against the power of those rigid forearms above him.

Again his arms flailed. His right arm knocked against something on the low table beside his chair. Instantly he realised what it was—and the thought sent a spasm of hope into his bursting brain.

Forcing his glance sideways, he fixed the position of the object—confirming that it was the whisky glass he had recently emptied.

Desperately grasping it, he smashed its rim down on the low table. The glass splintered—leaving a jagged, dangerous rim of projecting shards.

Gasping and violently writhing, he brought up the glass and stabbed its jagged rim right into the convulsed face above him. As the glass spikes tore into the flesh, he dragged the vicious weapon down the length of the contorted face.

Timothy screamed.

The ragged rips down his face opened out like a series of gaping lips. From each rip blood erupted.

The hands at Matthew's throat relaxed their grip. Frenziedly Matthew writhed himself free of their clutch.

While Timothy was raising the hands in a quick reflex to his maltreated face and blinded left eye, Matthew flung him off and scrambled clear—the now blood-rimmed glass still in his grasp.

On his feet, he turned, crouching with the glass jutting forward.

"Now!" he snarled. "Come on—let's see now if you can shut my mouth!"

Gibbering with pain, Timothy glowered at him between the fingers of the hands pressed to his tattered face. Blood trickled between the fingers and down the backs of the hands.

His voice choked with a corrosive hatred, he said balefully: "When you're going through it again you'll wish you were already dead!"

But even now he made no attempt to find a weapon to counter Matthew's. It was as if he regarded strangling as the natural gift—the natural use—of his hands. It did not even occur to him to kill by any other means.

Oblivious of everything but the raging lust to avenge his injuries and shut that dangerous mouth, he hurled himself at Matthew again—his hands reaching out for another disabling grip.

Matthew, though weakened from his recent ordeal and breathing in rasping gusts, met his brother halfway.

The jagged glass shards swept forward in an arc of menace. Timothy, panting too, evaded the weapon—and lunged past it with a speed Matthew now could not match.

Timothy got a grip on Matthew's left wrist. He tightened the grip—and twisted viciously. Matthew went down, dragging Timothy with him. The floor on which

Matthew had fought and killed his brother Alan became the arena of a bloody, more violent battle.

Timothy still had that grip on the left wrist, but Matthew still had the jagged glass. As the two men became locked in a furious, writhing, wrestling tangle, Matthew was stabbing away at random—every second or third stab finding a target on Timothy's ruined face.

The face was now a snarling mask of dripping, glistening red. But the pain only intensified Timothy's feral lust to kill.

From both men the thin veneer of civilisation had been sloughed off like the dead skin of a snake. They might have been two primitive sub-humans of pre-history, in a jungle world pre-dating the restraints of *homo sapiens*.

In a rolling tussle which momentarily kept his face safe from attack, Timothy got his free hand to Matthew's throat again. He secured a grip—and tightened it.

Again Matthew floundered. His teeth gleaming among the red mask, Timothy grinned exultantly. Quickly he transferred his other hand to the captured throat to reinforce his grip.

The two men continued to roll as that throttling grip sank deeper and deeper into the bruised flesh of the throat.

Both gasping huskily, they were quickly weakening from their frenzied exertions. Whenever Matthew got a glimpse of that hideous red-masked face he made another stab . . . but now the stabs were becoming slower, feebler, wilder.

Hanging on to the choking throat as the two bodies rolled and writhed, Timothy mouthed wordless snarls. Completely berserk, he fought like an animal with a death-grip that nothing could now dislodge.

He continued to fling Matthew's body about by that grip on the throat long after the body had become limp, resistless. Long after the lips of that dangerous mouth had become cyanosed, the gloated cheeks purple, the staring eyes glazed and the brain behind them dead.

It was only gradually that he realised Matthew no longer held the fearsome glass—that Matthew's body moved only under the impulsion of his murderer's superflous violence.

Slowly he released his grip and allowed the corpse to lie inert.

But, although he himself was now exhausted, his hatred was not fully vented, his venom not fully expressed.

Propped on his hands, which were shaking from the strain of the force he had exerted, he crouched wearily over his dead brother. Blood from his flayed face dripped down on the face of the dead man.

From the victor's snarling mouth came disjointed, gloating phrases . . . interrupted by spells when he had neither the breath nor the strength to speak.

From that red mask his febrile eyes glared down triumphantly at his victim.

"Did you think . . . you were a match for me . . . you bungler? . . . Even after you knew . . . I'd disposed of . . . that meddlesome brat . . . I threw in the pond . . . ? Even after you guessed . . . I'd also disposed of that . . . disgusting drunk . . . outside the pub . . . ?"

His chest rose and fell quickly to the hungry gasps of his breathing. But he found breath to go on.

". . . It took you . . . long enough . . . to guess who disposed of Alison . . . you bungler . . . That was funny . . . you frightening her . . . right into my hands. . . ."

His head drooped wearily, but still the gasping, gloating taunts came.

"You tried . . . to blackmail someone . . . right out of your own class. . . . You're not even . . . the first I've disposed of . . . this evening. . . . When I arrived here . . . I'd only just finished off . . . a luscious little French . . . *au pair* girl. . . . They'll be finding her

. . . in a day or two. . . . I'll have to . . . find a fresh . . . place for you. . . ."

He grinned down feebly at the dead face of his brother, now dappled with blood droppings from his own tattered face.

Preparatory to an effort to get to his feet, he looked up.

And then his eyes widened with fear and horror.

He had realised that Matthew's ears and brain had been dead and deaf to his taunting boasts.

But now he realised too that what he had gasped out had not gone unheard by someone other than himself.

There was a second pair of ears present which were neither deaf nor dead. And a brain which had absorbed all that mattered of his triumphant boasts of multi-murder.

In the doorway, staring in at this scene of fratricide—at the gory-faced killer crouching over his strangled brother—was Virgil Lodway.

In little more than a year, family history had repeated itself. For the second time the surgeon had walked in to find one of his sons slain by another son.

In his ashen face was the look of a man whose world had finally disintegrated beyond repair:

He said nothing. He just looked on in a terrible silence while his cold grey eyes took in every macabre detail of this second fratricide in his house.

Then he turned, stepped out of the room and disappeared.

Timothy tried to get up. But the shock and the frightening impact of discovery, on top of his strenuous physical efforts, had completed his exhaustion. He was a helpless mass of tremors when his father reappeared at the door.

And then the fear in the murderer's eyes intensified.

His father's face was as unmoving as Justice, as implacable as doom.

And the surgeon was carrying a gleaming-edged axe.

14: Expiation

TIMOTHY CRINGED.

Unhurriedly his father walked towards him, his face like sculptured stone. He came to a stop about four feet away from his crouching son. His last surviving son.

"So . . ." he said, in an expressionless, dehumanised voice, "this is the end. The end for you and the end for me."

"No!" Timothy grovelled at his feet. Keeping his eyes averted from the corpse beside him, he stared up at this man who had begotten both of them, the slain and the slayer.

"I heard it all," Virgil Lodway said stonily. "Even during your nightmare the other night I heard you shouting things which gave me hideous suspicions. Suspicions too hideous to entertain without absolute proof. Tonight I have heard—and seen—such proof!"

Timothy, abject on hands and knees, tried to speak. But no words would come.

Virgil Lodway looked down at the bloodstained guilty hands.

He said: "I knew a year ago that those hands I gave

you had committed murder. They strangled your brother Alan——"

The information made Timothy, even in his self-obsessed fear, stare up in dumb surprise.

"Despite that, I grafted them on to you. Like most people, I regarded hands as mere tools of the brain linked to them. Now I know better. You haven't possessed those hands. They have possessed *you*!"

Holding the axe at his side, he looked down bitterly at the last of his triplet sons. The son who had been his favourite.

"I know," he said, "that if you weren't exhausted from your murderous struggle you would now try to kill me too. Fortunately, I am able to do what must be done——"

Timothy now managed a husky babble.

"Father . . . I . . . don't . . . what are you going to . . ."

Virgil Lodway said bleakly: "This is no time for finesse. Nor is there any need of it. I gave you those hands—and it is I who must take them away. Now!"

Sliding his right hand midway along the haft of the axe, he pounced on his crouching son.

"*No . . . !*" Timothy shrieked in terror.

His shrieks and his feeble struggles were futile.

With the strength of all his disillusion, horror and despair, the surgeon captured one of his son's forearms and held it flat on the carpet. He held it motionless long enough for the axe to swing up and come crashing down on the extended wrist.

Timothy screamed with agony. But the axe rose and fell four more times—till the hand lay crudely severed and powerless on the bloodstained carpet.

In rhythm to the beat of the pumping heart, bright red blood spurted violently from the severed artery. But, with a veteran surgeon's inexcitability, Virgil Lodway grabbed the other forearm of his screaming son and pinned it down.

Again the axe rose and fell. This time only four strokes were sufficient. A second severed hand lay in gruesome isolation.

It was only now that the surgeon did anything to staunch the gouting blood. He laid aside the axe. With his own handkerchief and another he took from the groaning man's pocket, he expertly improvised two tourniquets.

When the blood had stopped spurting, he got to his feet and gazed down at his son, who now lay motionless from shock.

"I am not going to save you," he said. "But there are things I must say to you before you die."

From Timothy came whimpering moans, gradually growing weaker.

Ignoring them, the surgeon went on: "I've told you that those hands I gave you were guilty hands. The hands of a man who had murdered his brother. But, for the sake of your career and mine, I kept his wicked secret."

He gave a bitter smile. "Where are our careers now? This family is ended."

He paused. Then, incisively, he continued: "I gave you those guilty hands, and with them you have committed murders. Some people might say that Matthew's crime had left a curse on those hands. But you and I ought to have a more scientific explanation."

Semi-conscious from pain and shock, Timothy stared dully up at him.

"The explanation, I think," the surgeon said impersonally, as if in a lecture room at the university, "is in RNA. Ribo-nucleic acid.

"Do you remember us reading of the experiments made by Professor McConnell of Michigan University, with flat worms? A flat worm has a brain in its head. But if you teach it a trick and then cut the worm in halves, both halves know how to do the trick. The memory and aptitude, therefore, aren't confined to the brain.

"This was further proved when worms which had been trained to do a trick were cut up into pieces and fed to untrained worms. Afterwards the untrained worms would do the trick. It therefore seems that the aptitude was transferred in the tissue cells—probably in the RNA of the cells."

Gazing down at the last of his three sons, he said sombrely:

"It also seems that in grafting to your body the tissue of your guilty brother, I infected you with his homicidal urges. People speak of 'healing hands.' Those hands of his were killing hands, and with them you took over their murderous propensities. A murderer's RNA corrupted you."

The surgeon's face now showed his first overt signs of sorrow. But with it was an inexorable resolve.

"The fact that those hands were able to control you shows that you had completely absorbed their contamination. You are corrupted beyond cure. Your crimes have to be expiated. Innocent people have died because of your taint—and you too must die."

Gaunt from the strain he was undergoing, Virgil Lodway stooped over the son he had condemned.

Deliberately he untied one tourniquet and wrenched it off. Then the other. Straightening up, he stood aside and watched his son bleed to death.

Timothy had been dead several minutes when the doorbell rang. Virgil Lodway was deaf to the repeated ringing.

He remained engrossed with his dead while two tall men entered the hall and came to the lighted doorway of the lounge.

It was their hoarse exclamations of horror which aroused him.

His eyes brilliant from the mental anguish consuming

him, he turned to face them. One of them was a man he had already met. Inspector Russell of the Stilford C.I.D.

Coming almost nervously into the room, the two intruders looked at the final macabre tableau. The corpse with black-gloved artificial hands. The bloodied drinking-glass. The red-edged axe. The corpse with no hands at all.

And the hands which had been hacked from it. . . .

In a voice remote and glacial, Virgil Lodway said: "Any crime committed by those hands earlier than a year ago must have been committed by my son Matthew there." He pointed to the corpse with black gloves. "He murdered his brother Alan."

Ignoring the exclamations of astonishment, he redirected his gaze, now sombre again, to the body without hands.

Standing among the wreckage of his life, he said: "I take the blame for all the crimes since committed by my other son Timothy here. Because I grafted on to him the murderous corruption of those vile things!"

He pointed to the two severed hands with their club-tipped thumbs.

The hands of Cain.